THE BLUE OCEAN'S DAUGHTER

There was a flash of the priming.   The pistol hung fire.

The Blue Ocean's Daughter

BY

CYRUS TOWNSEND BRADY

*Author of "Richard the Brazen," "The Corner in Coffee,"
"The Southerners," etc.*

ILLUSTRATED

NEW YORK
MOFFAT, YARD & COMPANY
1913

TO MY VALUED FRIEND

ALSOP LEFFINGWELL

CONTENTS

v

vi   *CONTENTS*

LIST OF ILLUSTRATIONS

CHAPTER I

THE LETTER-OF-MARQUE

A FEW words preliminary, if you please, gentle reader! A ship, a woman, men! Here are all the elements of a story. The vessel with its cargo of illusions; the woman, the focus of events; the men woven in the tangled web!

The ocean lends itself to romance! It has life, it moves, it has personality. The water is quick and the shore is dead. With that personality the bark, driven by the wind and tempest-tossed, is imbued. Even the hideous, monstrous, misshapen iron pot of to-day, "skyhooting through the brine," has an attraction of its own, although its charm pales before that of the oaken-timbered, tall-masted, wide-sparred, canvas-covered sea-bird of the olden time. So that the ship and the sea are proper backgrounds—curious that the earthly word should here slip in—for the story about to be related.

Now, there have been romances without

women and stories of deep and abiding interest in which they played no part, as witness the story of Joseph, if we leave out Madam Potiphar. But there are not many, and most romances are built about the eternal feminine in one or the other of the multifarious guises in which she presents herself to that elemental animal, man. While there may be romances for men without women, however, there are none for women without men. Here you have a trio, therefore, which promise much. To repeat: a ship, a woman, and men. So much by way of introduction.

Let us descend to earth and feel under our feet the solid substratum of the deck-plank. Give me a tumbling, heaving, tossing bark rather than all the mountains that were stayed on the foundations of the earth before the waters of the Great Deep broke forth. Dare I, after this prelude, say that the ship in question upon which is to be played the comedy, the tragedy and the romance of this veracious tale rejoiced in, or struggled along despite the double name, *Hiram and Susan.*

It is not alone a Howard, or a Montmorency, or a De Guzman, or a Hapsburg that spell romance. There was a love story, therefore, that attached itself to the *Hiram and Susan.* A love story of the past, and by the way, being past, it has nothing to do with this love story. There, I have deliberately let the secret out. It is a love story. If you are tired of that kind in these days of problem and other novels only to be characterized fitly by uglier words that indicate the contents, put this one down, for there is no problem here but that which began with the Garden of Eden and which is involved in the way of a man with a maid, and eke, the way of a maid with a man.

Do not look at the last page. I assure you that this story ends happily. I have written but one book that ended badly and I have been sorry for it ever since—besides, it did not sell. Well, then, to our story.

As idle as the proverbial painted ship upon the proverbial painted ocean they lay, which does not mean that the ship was still, although there was no breeze.

The *Hiram and Susan,* and her pursuer as well, a half a league away, out of gunshot astern and to windward, were rolling back and forth with long, deliberate, sluggish motions, under the influence of that heaving swell which is rarely absent from the ocean, no matter how profound the calm.

An observer midway between the two ships would have seen not a sign of life about either of them. Yet, if he could have stood on the decks of first one and then the other he would have been amazed at the scene of activity before him.

In the minds of the men of the *Hiram and Susan* was all the fear of the pursued, and in the minds of the men of the other ship all the zeal and lust of the pursuer. A stern chase is a long chase, and this one had been going on for several days amid baffling airs and alternating periods of calm.

If anything, the pursuer had gained and weathered on the pursued, but their positions, relatively, had changed little since the morning of two days before, when the rising sun suddenly disclosed to the watchers on the smaller vessel the larger ship close at hand. Each captain had used all the skill and seamanship that his experience suggested. Both were past masters of the art, and the change in relative positions, therefore, indicated the qualities of the two ships.

The light variable winds which had prevailed had at last definitely abandoned that section of the ocean, and the most weather-wise could see no promise of a breeze. It was in the nature of events that the crews of the two ships should have been as idle as their vessels, and that they were busy indicated the nature of the exigency. Unless the night brought wind it would inevitably, in the judgment of the captain of the *Hiram and Susan,* bring danger.

The ships were near enough for a boat expedition, and the *Hiram and Susan* was a sufficiently valuable prize to risk much for the gaining.

Therefore, while the men on the big frigate were busily laying plans for a cutting-out expedition the men on the smaller ship were equally energetic in preparing for their reception.

It was about sunset, and the older and more experienced sailors on the merchantman realized that if the attack came at all it would come soon. In default of boarding-nettings, lines were run between the shrouds at short intervals, which would offer some obstacle to a man attempting to clamber up the sides of the ship.

The five guns on each broadside which constituted the armament of the *Hiram and Susan,* and the longer gun on the high topgallant forecastle, were cast loose and provided. The arm-chests were broken open and the men supplied with cutlass and pistol.

Captain Hiram Hubbell and his zealous and

energetic mate, one Owen Conant, of Nantucket, a gigantic New Englander, consulted together and made every preparation for the expected attack, they could think of.

Even the Spanish cook and his boy, Manuel, were busy in heating caldrons of water. Bars of iron and other heavy articles were arranged amidships, handy to either side.

When all had been done the men were given their suppers and were ordered to turn in on the spar-deck, so that in case of an alarm they could be immediately called to action. Owing to the seriousness of the situation, the mate went forward to keep watch on the forecastle while the captain remained on the high, old-fashioned poop which balanced the topgallant forecastle.

Here and there appointed seamen of the watch kept their feet along the gangways, and as night came, the little group moved about among the sleepers in the waist, with every faculty alert for the slightest indication of an approaching enemy.

There was no moon, and the warm, thick haze obscured even the stars. The night was as black as pitch; there was not a light showing on the ship; even the lantern over the binnacle aft, where the compass swung, was carefully hooded. The ship was making no way, and

there were no hands at the wheel, which was secured amidships by a light lashing.

Captain Hiram paced softly up and down with
the catlike tread of the veteran seaman, from one
side of the poop-deck to the other, and then aft,
peering about him anxiously in every direction.
He was not alone in his watch. A slight and
slender figure paced by his side, and with eyes
more youthful and brilliant strove to see what
was hid from the glances of the weather-beaten
sailor.

Twenty years before, another figure had thus
and often paced by the side of Captain Hiram
Hubbell, master and owner of the stanch merchant ship, *Hiram and Susan*. He often thought
of it, especially when he walked the deck with
this slender stripling touching his arm.

The *Hiram and Susan* represented a dual
partnership. If the term were admissible I
might say a double dual partnership, with one
constant factor and two independent variables.
It happens, without in the least reflecting upon
their character, that the one constant factor was
a man and the two independent variables were
of the other sex. One of the variables died in
giving birth to the other, and may, therefore,
save for a brief retrospective glance, be eliminated from the equation.

She yielded up her life on the ship that bore her name in conjunction with that of her young husband, who was both master and half owner. The other half she herself had held in fee simple, because by the aid of her dowry which paid half the cost, the *Hiram and Susan* had been built. A premature delivery, on a return voyage from England taken during the pleasant summer months in the hope of benefiting the health of Susan the First and preparing her for the strain of maternity, had brought to life Susan the Second. The event had occurred in latitude 40° 42′ and longitude 45° 15′ exactly, by observation taken by the mate at eight bells, while the captain was below in the cabin performing the delicate duties of accoucheur, a function to which his unskilled hands lent themselves unreadily and with consequences disastrous to his wife.

Three days after, with all the solemnity of the Prayer Book service, they committed the body of the first Susan to the Great Deep, there to await the general resurrection of the dead. As the canvas-clad, shot-weighted figure flashed whitely from the gratings and plunged into the blue of the fathomless seas, lapping softly the sides of the ship as if in tender and soothing sympathy, while the mate read those mournful words with which humanity is so familiar, the first partnership between Hiram and Susan was broken.

Life is a succession of relationships. We go constantly from the old to the new. Captain Hiram Hubbell standing on the quarterdeck, choking back his grief, manlike, lest it show before the huddle of men grouped forward, and holding in his arms a bundle swathed in a new pea-jacket, having brought the baby there from a feeling that the first Susan might have wished it; with the idea, perhaps, that the lone woman in the hammock on the grating might feel more at ease among the men from the presence of the little woman in the pea-jacket in his arms—Captain Hubbell, I say, having thought all this, straightway entered upon another partnership with another and a smaller Susan whose sharp cries were coincident with the tolling of the bell forward. And so as one Voyage of Life ended, another was begun.

The *Hiram and Susan* sailed on across many seas, during many voyages, generally containing two skippers in the cabin, the captain of the ship and a wee and winsome maiden, growing taller and stronger and braver and sweeter with every passing cruise. The affection that existed between old Hiram and young Susan was one of those that pass the observer's understanding.

There had not been a bolder sailor, or a braver man, or a more tender heart, sailing out of Massachusetts Bay than Hiram Hubbell when he wooed and won Susan Andersen. And the affection he had lavished on the wife he soon transferred to the daughter. The great Doctor Johnson was of the opinion that no man would go to sea who had wit enough to contrive to get himself cast into prison. Quoting from memory, that sentence lacks the ponderosity of the sententious Doctor's oracular deliverances, but the meaning is clear. Hubbell did not agree with Doctor Johnson, of whom, by the way, he and most people alive at that time had heard little, if anything.

Honest Hiram came of sturdy yeoman stock. His forefathers, if they had not been among the tremendously inclusive and prolific number who crowded the *Mayflower,* were nevertheless among the forerunners of the men who made Massachusetts Bay vie with Virginia in the spirit, the enterprise and the liberty-loving characteristics of its citizens. He had been educated, not to the limit of his capacity, but to the limit of his willingness, by his father, who would have been glad to see him succeed to his extensive business as a merchant and a shipowner. But Hiram Hubbell had no fancy for the counting-house. The heaving deck, the soughing of the wind through the rigging, the buffet of the waves against the bow—these were life to him.

He had run away from Harvard College in his sophomore year. On his return from his first cruise, his family had made a virtue of necessity and put him in the way of advancement in his chosen profession. He had earned the money that he put into the *Hiram and Susan* as a sailor and master of one of his father's ships, by doing such wise trading on his own account as was allowed by the customs of the time.

He had earned more than money, too, for in one of his infrequent periods of life ashore he had taken Susan Andersen to wife. She, too, came of good New England stock on her mother's side; hence the Susan. Her father had been a Dane. She had Viking blood and a common interest drew husband and wife toward the sea.

The young Susan that was left him after that white splash in the water alluded to, was like her mother and Captain Hiram thanked God for it every time he looked upon her. She had the blue eyes and bright hair and vivid color of the Northland, and he loved and cherished her the more in that she showed no trace of his own dark and somewhat swarthy visage.

The sailor is popularly supposed of necessity to be as rude as that Boreas whose bluster he proverbially antagonizes. Captain Hiram was not that kind of a seaman. The touch of things high and holy which had been his during his brief married life, the refining influences of a mighty love ending in a great sorrow, as had the mightiest of all loves ever recorded; the sweet association with helpless innocence, the careful watch over the development of young Susan, the delightful comradeship with so much that was beautiful and lovely, had sweetened and softened the spirit of the man. Unconsciously, his effort had been not merely to command ships and men, but to master a man, himself, that he might make life wholesome and sweet and pleasant to the little shipmate of his maturer years, and that he might make her wholesome and sweet and pleasant in it. Oh, mistake me not! His love for his daughter had not weakened him. No love that is worth anything fails to strengthen man. It was love that endured the Cross and despised the shame, that made such endurance and contempt possible.

Captain Hiram lost none of his manliness in the life struggle on the seas. He studied to make himself worthy and able to teach and train his quick and responsive daughter. He had kept his daughter at sea with him during by far the greater part of her life. The results of his educational experiment, while not entirely disappointing, were what might have been expected from a plain but honest man's attempt to bring up a woman in the companionship of men alone. Nothing on earth—or sea—could ever disturb the femininity of Susan Hubbell, and yet in an age when delicacy was esteemed the chief charm of woman—bodily delicacy, that is, not mental or spiritual—Susan Hubbell belonged, if the phrase be admissible, to a subsequent generation.

She was entirely unacquainted with the social life of the women of her time, when to be fashionable it was necessary to faint on every and any occasion, and when the vapors was the prevalent feminine disease. She had no skill in the polite accomplishments of the day; indeed, no knowledge of them or of her lack of them. Captain Hiram had kept the girl sweet and pure, guarding her as jealously as the angel at the gate protected Paradise from trespass by the sons of Adam.

He had taught her, in addition to what book learning he had at command, all the nice art of the sailor. At both fore-and-aft and quarter-deck seamanship she was proficient. She could hand and reef and steer. She could pass the weather earring and tack the ship. Indeed, she could handle the *Hiram and Susan* with the skill and facility of her captain. Old and battered tars had showed her how to ply the needle with the same deftness they themselves exhibited. The few books in the cabin of the *Hiram and Susan*—and the flood of books had not begun in those days—she had carefully read and digested. She had picked up a smattering of French and knew the Lingua Franca of the Mediterranean thoroughly.

She was an unerring shot with small arms, and was her father's master in the somewhat rude sword-play which he had taught her. Her strength and physical activity would not be so much remarked in these days of vigorous outdoor womanhood, but then they were surprising.

Her instinctive feminine qualities had not been entirely eradicated, either. Indeed, some of them had been enhanced by the life she led. She was tall and straight and strong, inured to all such athletic exercises as may be practiced on a ship. She was as graceful as any woman on earth, although she had never learned to dance, or play the harpsichord, and could not ride a horse, and did not know one card in the deck from another. She could talk fluently and well upon serious subjects, but small gossip was utterly foreign to her. And she could sing like a wild bird, with a power and sweetness in her rich contralto voice that only lacked training to be enthralling.

Frequently, one might almost say habitually, when cruising on the *Hiram and Susan* she wore the ordinary dress of a sailor. She wore it without consciousness of immodesty or impropriety, almost without thought of it. It was convenient, and it suited her. If she had had other standards by which to measure herself she might have appreciated the situation better.

Yet she was withal a very woman. Not even the coarse garments of the sailor lad as she stood lightly poised upon the heaving deck of the *Hiram and Susan* on this certain night in the late spring of the year of our Lord, 1782, could disguise it. Her beauty would have told the tale if nothing else; albeit it was beauty male-clad and full-armed, like an ancient goddess.

Of course, Miss Susan Hubbell had been loved by many men, but they were mostly the rough sailors, the mates and officers, of her father's ship. None of them had the least power to awaken the most fugitive emotions in her heart, and the present mate, Mr. Owen Conant, was not more successful than the others.

Love, when it came, would be a great awakening
to her.

The father and daughter conversed in low
tones as they paced the weary watch. It was
significant of Susan's capacities that as they
tramped to and fro on the deck her father often
felt the touch of steel impinging against him,
which showed that the belt she wore carried pistols and a cutlass. If need arose he was sure that
she would use them well.

There were only thirty in the crew of the
Hiram and Susan, which since the beginning of
the war had carried a letter-of-marque. Captain
Hiram Hubbell was a peaceful trader, but he
was not above picking up the windfalls that fortune cast athwart his prow, and with the thrift
of his ancestry he had already added consider-
ably to the sea ventures of his ordinary trade by
taking several small vessels belonging to the
British, and he had fought one smart brush with
a rather heavier privateer of the enemy, which
he had successfully beaten off.

The long course of the war, which had
dragged on through seven years, had told
heavily upon American seamen, and the present
crew of the merchantman had been recruited
mainly in Bordeaux, whence the last lading had
been taken, and a more rascally crowd of black-

guards and cutthroats Captain Hiram had never commanded.

"Needs must when there are no others," he thought philosophically, and he determined that before the ship reached Boston he would have tamed some of the more turbulent spirits and let them know what it was to have a master.

For the same reason, it had been difficult to get officers, and the *Hiram and Susan* had sailed with but three.

One of them, the second mate, had gone with the best men in a small prize which had been captured the week before. This left the captain and the first mate, Conant, who was eminently fitted for some higher command, but who had remained attached to the ship for several years because he was even more attached to the ship-master's daughter.

Under such circumstances the boatswain would have been called upon to take a watch, but the best candidate who had presented himself for this position at Bordeaux had been a Frenchman, whose name, on this cruise, was François.

He was a good enough seaman, a handsome, devil-may-care sort of fellow, who concealed beneath his grace and pleasant address as black a heart as ever filled the human bosom. What his career had been, what his history, Captain

Hiram did not know. He shrewdly surmised, however, after a few days' intercourse with the man, that there were dark passages in his life which nobody would be permitted to learn if the boatswain could help it.

Only a certain quality of authority which the man possessed that made him a valuable influence in controlling his rascally crew had enabled Captain Hiram to tolerate him at all, but he was the best man forward of the mast, undoubtedly, in an assemblage in which Greeks and Levantines and other foreigners made up the majority, and the captain kept him there.

So far, however, there had been no open outbreak upon the part of the boatswain.

Indeed, for a certain reason he had striven to gain the favor of his superior. With a high idea of his own powers of pleasing, and with an utter indifference to the relative stations of himself and the captain's daughter, he had plainly striven to ingratiate himself with the latter, somewhat to Susan's amusement, more to her disgust.

Susan, who entered fully into her father's difficulties and perplexities, had refrained from disclosing the fact that the boatswain had presumed to make advances to her. She felt abundantly able to take care of herself, and there was not the slightest reason for annoying Captain Hiram with such a recital. His anger would have been fearful indeed, and he would have wreaked it to the full upon the boatswain.

It was the day of the cat-o'-nine-tails, and Susan had no doubt that her father would cause François to be flogged half to death. This would serve no purpose save to turn a latent into an active enemy, and with the crew then on board the *Hiram and Susan* it was a possibility not to be sneered at.

Indeed, it was quite evident that should the expected boat-attack be made that night from the British frigate to windward it could only be repulsed by the united efforts of every man on the ship. Therefore, adding to her other good qualities of a manly stamp the fine art of reticence, Susan said nothing.

For a long time the few awake on the trader kept careful watch, but it was not until five bells in the first watch that anything happened.

CHAPTER II

BOARDERS AWAY

"Is that a breeze I feel?" said Captain Hiram, suddenly stopping in his ceaseless pace of the deck.

"I think not, father," answered his daughter.

The old captain wetted his finger and lifted it, seeking to feel a coolness from a draft of air.

Susan, whose faculties were exceedingly keen, threw her head up, and listened for the breeze.

"I feel something," said the captain.

" 'Tis only the disturbance in the air caused by the rocking of the ship, I think," returned his daughter.

"Aye, that'll be it, and I hope it will be the only disturbance in the air we——"

"Listen!"

Susan had not heard the breeze, but her quick ear had caught another sound. The night was very still. During the pauses between the slatting of the sails, the creaking of the timbers, and the sway of the loose rigging, she thought she had detected a faint, creaking noise as of oars in rowlocks.

"What is it?" asked the sailor, softly.

Susan's voice sank to a whisper, more from the excitement of the moment than from any necessity.

"There!" She pointed out into the thick darkness. "Don't you hear it? Oars! They are coming! Call the men."

"Wait!" said Captain Hiram. He did not wish to awaken the majority of the crew without being certain: "Are you sure?" he asked, straining in vain to hear.

"Absolutely," returned the girl. "It is there." She pointed off to starboard. Then she turned. "Why, no; now it seems to come from the other side. Call the men," she urged, excitement beginning to tell upon her.

"Patience!" returned her cool old father. "If it is the boats, they'll give louder notice presently, and we'll have time. Everything is ready, and I don't want to waken the men on what may be a false alarm."

"It isn't a false alarm," persisted the girl, sharply. "There! Didn't you hear that?"

"Aye," returned the captain, his ear having caught a heavier thump where perhaps the muffling had slipped from an oar. "It's to star-board."

He walked over to starboard quickly, put his hand behind his ear, and leaned far out over the rail. This time he caught the faint sound more plainly.

"That'll be it," he said, turning to Susan. "It's boats for certain."

"Can we beat them off?" asked the girl, her pulses dancing.

"I don't know," answered her father. "If I had some good Americans on the decks, there, we might, but with this crowd of half-breeds——"

"They are nearer. You can hear them more plainly now," interrupted the girl.

At that instant one of the men in the waist came running aft with soft, stealthy, noiseless steps. He stopped at the break of the poop.

"There's something moving out yonder, sir; boats, I take it," he said quietly.

"I know. Wake up the men. Tell them not to make a sound as they value their lives. They know what to do. Get them to the starboard battery, but no firing till I give the word."

"Aye, aye, sir," said the man, turning instantly about his task.

In a moment figures of recumbent men could

be dimly seen rising from the decks and slipping noiselessly to their stations in the gloom.

"Ought we to show a light?" asked Susan, with eager interest.

"What! and tell them where we are, and what to shoot at, and how to get aboard? No, indeed," returned her father.

"I didn't think of that," said the girl.

"Now, do you stay here a moment," returned the veteran seaman, "and I'll take a look along the decks. Sing out if you notice anything."

He ran rapidly down the ladder and passed from gun to gun, seeing that all was ready, stopping a moment to exchange a word or two with Mr. Conant and the huddle of men around the long-tom on the forecastle, and then made his way aft to the poop, where Susan had been nervously watching. She could do most things that a man could do, and many of them better than most men, but she had never been in action before, and something of the woman was naturally uppermost.

Her father laid his hand upon her arm and felt it tremble.

"My girl," he said considerately, "you had better go below. There's going to be bloody work on these decks, and you will be safer in the cable tiers."

"I will never do it! Never!" cried Susan. "I will take my part here with the rest."

"But——"

"Father, don't make me."

It was wrong, of course, but there was something in the girl's plea that touched the brave sailor's heart, especially as he had some doubts of his ability to keep his daughter down in the cable tiers once he got her there. After all, there would be little danger on the poop-deck, he thought quickly, if he could contrive to make her remain there.

"Very well," he said, after some reflection; "I will let you stay on deck on condition that you give me your word of honor not to leave the poop. Indeed, I shall have to be with the men, and I shall want some one here to keep watch and give the alarm."

"I give you my word," said the girl, man-like extending her hand.

Caresses were rare between these two, but this time the old sailor drew her to his breast, kissed her fondly, patted her on the shoulder gently, and murmured a prayer ere he released her.

Having thus discharged his paternal and religious duties, he loosened his cutlass from its sheath, examined, by feeling, the brace of pistols, and bade Susan do likewise.

The noise of the approaching boats was nearer now, and quite perceptible, although the oars had been skilfully muffled and were handled cautiously by practised hands, and no human sounds were made. The approach of such a number of boats and men, however, could not longer be concealed.

"They'll give tongue in a minute," said the old man to his daughter. "Aye, there," he continued, as a sudden flash of light lanced the darkness, followed by the roar of a piece of boat artillery and the singing of a shot uselessly whirled across the deck.

"At her, lads! We'll take her out of hand," a sharp voice called out.

A burst of cheering rose from the water below. Straining eyes on the *Hiram and Susan* fancied they could make out the boats.

Not a sound had been made by them, however, but the stillness was now broken by a thunderous discharge.

"Keep fast," roared Captain Hiram. "Who fired that gun?"

"I did," answered a voice out of the obscurity.

"Damn you, François!" cried Hubbell. "I'll settle with you for this."

"Here they come," cried another voice out of the darkness.

"Fire! Fire!" shouted Captain Hiram, furiously angry.

The four remaining guns and the long-tom roared out an instant response. The battery was largely fired at random, but the captain thought he detected a crash of timbers, and he was sure that mingled with the cheers and yells were shrieks of pain.

"Hold your small-arm fire, boys," he cried. "Give them the cold steel first, if they try to board us. Stand by!"

The next instant a boat crashed amidships against the *Hiram and Susan*. Men stood up in the stern-sheets and fired directly at the rail. One of the crew had incautiously exposed himself, and fell back with a bullet in his brain.

Under cover of this discharge a dozen men from the fore-sheets of the boat scrambled to the gangway; cutlasses upraised they swarmed the side of the ship. At the same instant another boat hooked on beneath the fore-chains and one touched the ship by the main-chains. The marines in the stern-sheets of the boats opened fire, and the sailors forward swarmed in the chains.

The first Britisher who showed himself through the gangway was shot dead. The next man gained a footing in the opening, and cutlasses clashed viciously. The men in the main-chains scrambled over the side, but, led by Captain Hiram in person, the crew threw themselves upon this group and drove them back against the pin-rail and held them there, fighting desperately.

The attack in the fore-chains was not quite so successful, for Mr. Conant, on the forecastle, swung a lantern over the side, and by means of that light, which gave him a fair view of the assailants, he and his men deliberately picked off the men swarming into the chains. The boat, held to the ship by a boat-hook, drifted aft till the man holding her alongside was shot, when it brought to, against the boat in the main-chains.

This was the easiest access to the ship, since four or five of the English were already on deck and the boarders would not be shot or stabbed as they climbed over the rail. So the officer in charge of the boats, who maintained a cool head and seemed to be a man of skill, directed the men from the second boat to reenforce the attacking party in the main-chains.

Catching hold of every available rope, stay, or shroud, they swarmed up the side of the ship like monkeys. The rail was black with them. A volley from the pistols of the crew laid some of them low, but others gained the deck. At the same time, the attack in the gangway was pushed home more vigorously, and for a moment the fate of the ship trembled in the balance. The air was filled with shouts and cries, with shrieks and curses, and the night sang with the grating crash of steel on steel, punctuated by the sharper detonation of pistol-shots.

Seeing the forecastle neglected, Mr. Conant gathered his handful and ran along the gangways toward the mainmast. To dispose of the attack in the waist was not difficult. A piece of pig-iron ballast weighing perhaps two hundred and fifty pounds lay in the lee of the boom-boats opposite the open gang-way. The mate had put it there himself.

He picked it up as if it had been a paving-stone, and stepping to the gang-way, lifted it high above his head and crashed it down into the overloaded boat below him.

The heavy iron bar went through the bottom of the boat as if it that had been made of paper. She began to fill at once. Those of her crew who could do so scrambled aboard the other two boats lying abreast of each other near the main chains, while the hapless wounded, vainly praying for help, drifted away and sank in the darkness.

Mr. Conant then joined the men who had

united forces with Captain Hiram's party, and the attack on the English was pressed home with vigor. Slowly but surely they were forced to give back, and the ship was almost cleared when above the noise of the tumult a woman's shriek rent the air.

CHAPTER III

THE ATTACK THAT FAILED

CAPTAIN HIRAM heard that scream; Mr. Conant heard it; and so, too, did big François. Captain Hiram surmised that the enemy were attacking the poop, but he did not dare to leave the group on the quarter-deck. They were on the verge of retreat, and to weaken the pressure upon them for a minute would be to give them the ship.

"Conant! François!" he shouted, while vigorously belaboring a British sailor with his sword. "To the poop with you. Miss Susan!"

Mr. Conant, however, could not answer to the appeal. A gigantic Cornishman had grappled with him bear-fashion, and the two were wrestling about the decks like wild beasts, forgetful of everything but the immediate fury of personal combat.

François, who had been none too active in the fray, did respond. He turned and ran up the ladder to the poop-deck.

The British attack had been cleverly planned. A fourth boat had made a wide détour, and had hooked on to the stern in the midst of the battle; rightly judging that, since the stern was the most inaccessible place from the water—the high poop had been noted from the British ship —it would be lightly guarded at best, and that probably no one would be there, since the natural tendency would be to draw every one to the main defense in the waist.

Through some oversight, the Jacob's-ladder which usually trailed over the stern of such ships had not been lifted.

The British coming softly alongside, unheard by Susan, who was indeed straining her eyes at the huddle of the black forms forward, congratulated themselves upon this as a great piece of good fortune. It did not prove so, however, for in the end it was their undoing.

Only one man at a time could climb up the Jacob's-ladder. If they had come along under the mizzen-chains and made their way aboard that way, as they had intended, a swarm would have gained the poop-deck before anything could have been done by its solitary occupant, and the ship would have been irretrievably lost. But the dangling Jacob's ladder was too tempting. They took the line of least resistance generally fatal in warfare and in love.

A half-naked sailor, his cutlass between his teeth, his pistols loose in his belt, scrambled up the ladder, as many as could get on it following him.

Something—some noise, some premonition— at the instant his head appeared above the deck, drew Susan's glance backward. A flash from a pistol discharged far on the forward deck was luckily reflected on the bright blade of the man's sword for a second. He had got his left hand over the rail, and had his sword in his right. It was another attack, and the safety of her father, the ship, the men, depended upon her!

She held her pistol in one hand and her sword in the other, ready for any emergency. Without thought, she bounded across the deck, and with the wild cry which her father had heard, she struck at the man's head with her cutlass, forgetting the more effective weapon, the pistol, and thrust at him again and again, screaming with excitement. The man, with oaths and curses, strove to protect himself with his sword, but he was taken at too great a disadvantage. Although Susan for the moment lost all her skill and science at sword-play, one of her random blows got home in his shoulder. She felt, with a sickening emotion, the resistance offered by human flesh to the thrust of a sword. The man screamed, threw up his hands, and as the woman pressed upon him, fell backward yelling with pain.

The Jacob's-ladder was swarming with men, and as he went down he carried the whole number with him, some of them into the sea, others into the boat.

Susan stood appalled. The next instant a tall figure loomed out of the darkness beside her.

"You have driven them over!" he cried. "Your pistols?"

Without a word Susan handed them to him. He leaned over the rail and fired point-blank into the huddled mass in the boat. A scattering volley hastily aimed and doing no damage was the answer, and a moment later the boat drifted away in the darkness.

"*Sacrè bleu!*" cried the sailor, "you have saved us all. It was well done. You are a woman in a thousand."

They were alone on the quarter-deck. He slipped his arm around her waist, and before she knew what he was doing, he kissed her full upon the lips. Susan, infuriated, wrenched herself free and drove at him with her sword, but François was too near for her to use the weapon effectively.

He easily caught her wrist with his hand and held her powerless.

"Forgive me!" he said, "but I love you. I am a great man in my own land. For love of you I have come on this ship."

"You coward! You dog!" cried Susan, wrenching her hand away.

"Father!" she screamed loudly.

"Stop!" hissed the Frenchman. "If you tell him, I will kill him. The crew are with me. Mark you."

"What is it?" cried Captain Hiram, springing up on the poop.

"We have driven them away from the poopdeck, captain," said François, with quiet presence of mind, stepping forward as he spoke, "thanks to the courage of your daughter."

"Thank God!" returned Captain Hiram, fervently; "and we've repulsed them from the waist. Go forward, François; the ship is clear of the British dogs."

"Will they come back again?" asked Susan.

"Not to-night, after what we have given them, I think," answered the captain. "One boat sunk, a dozen Britishers who came on board and didn't get back, some of them taken, the rest killed, and Heaven only knows how many wounded in the attack. For a set of peaceful traders, I think we have done very well. You screamed, Susan. It almost took the heart out of me when I heard it. What was it?"

"Another boat was there. They swarmed up the Jacob's-ladder. I saw them and—and—I drove the first man down. I think he fell and cleared the ladder."

"You saved the ship. Who came to your assistance?"

"François did. He discharged my two pistols into the boat, and then——"

"And then what?" asked her father.

Susan hesitated. Was the threat of the boatswain true or not? Were the crew disaffected, and did he have them in hand? Would danger result to her father?

"What is it?" insisted Captain Hiram, who was not without his suspicions."

"Will you give me your word to do nothing until morning?"

"Why, of course. I am not likely to do anything now. We have to watch the ship, and —— Well, what is it?"

"He seized me in his arms. He kissed me. He said he loved me."

"The hound!" cried the captain, starting forward. "I'll have him flogged until he can't crawl to your feet to beg your pardon."

"Not to-night," said Susan.

"This moment," roared the captain.

"You promised," said the girl. "He swore that the crew were disaffected."

"They fought like men to-night."

"Aye, but that was to save their lives, and perhaps their ship."

"My ship," returned Captain Hiram.

"Yours now, but theirs to-morrow if you don't——"

"How dare he, the low cur!"

"Quite so, but you must do nothing to-night. You mustn't even refer to it. You promised me."

"Aye, aye, I'll keep my word," said the captain. "We've done enough to-night."

He turned and stepped to the break of the poop.

"Men," he cried, "you have done well. I don't think they'll trouble us to-night again, but we'll keep a sharp lookout, and if they do, they'll find us ready for them, as we were before. Manuel!"

"Here, sir," returned the Spanish boy.

"Open the lazaretto and serve out a good tot of grog all round, let all hands splice the main-brace, and if any of you are hurt report on the quarter-deck at once and we'll see what can be done for you. Mr. Conant!"

"Aye, aye, sir."

"Will you muster the crew and report to me any casualties?"

"Yes, sir," answered the mate, and the next moment his deep voice could be heard calling the roll of the men.

Two of the Americans had been killed, three had been seriously wounded, and a number had received slight and inconsequent bruises. On the whole, they had come off very well.

The seriously wounded were taken into the forecastle and their wounds attended to by Captain Hiram and Susan.

Then the captain peremptorily ordered the girl to turn in. He only succeeded in enforcing obedience to his command by promising faithfully to call her in case another attack was made, and, indeed, he was the more willing to give that promise, for, as he said to her:

"It was you who saved the ship. If you had not been on the poop and stopped that attack to larboard we would have been overpowered. We had all we could do in the waist, and a fresh party on our backs would have ended everything. You are the bravest and best girl I ever saw, and a true daughter of an American sailor."

He drew her to him again and kissed her, with another prayer of thanksgiving this time, and dismissed her for the night.

CHAPTER IV

A TASTE OF THE CAT

THE next morning found the relative positions of the two ships still unchanged. Unless the wind sprang up, giving one or the other the advantage, the people on the *Hiram and Susan* had little to fear from their pursuers. The night boat-attack having failed, it would be madness to attempt a similar maneuver in the daytime. There was nothing for either ship to do, apparently, but play the waiting game, yet Captain Hiram had business of importance.

At the first streak of daylight he had called all hands. The arms of the men had been stowed in the chests, which had been locked, and Mr. Conant had the keys in his pocket. The captain and the mate were both armed, as usual, with sword and pistols, so that, backed by the moral force of their authority and position, they could dominate the crew.

The men had scarcely mustered on the quar-

ter-deck before Susan came from the cabin and
joined the two officers. She, too, was armed.
There were six pistols and three swords against
a score or more of men armed with sheath-
knives. The six pistols and three swords also
were on the raised poop, towering six feet above
the quarter-deck. Susan noticed as she joined
her father, that the evidences of the conflict had
been removed, so far as possible.

Indeed, there were practically no evidences.
The bloody decks had been swabbed up; the
dead bodies of the enemy thrown overboard and
those of the crew taken forward. Save for cut
lines and here and there a splintered rail, the
ship looked much as she always did. The guns
had been secured, and one ignorant of the
events of the night would not have imagined
anything had happened were it not for the sullen
looks of the crew.

At the head of them all stood the boatswain,
his arms folded, a look of mocking defiance on
his lips.

"Men," began Captain Hiram shortly, "I told
you last night that you had done well. You beat
off the British handsomely, and a month's extra
pay goes to each man when we get to Boston
Harbor."

No cheers greeted this remark, which, greatly

to the surprise of the captain, was received in ominous silence.

Captain Hiram went on grimly:

"When I said you have done well, I wish to make an exception of one man."

He paused significantly.

"And who is that, pray?" asked François, impudently.

"You," said the captain, curtly.

"And what did I do?"

"You insulted my daughter, here, last night."

"If to love your daughter," began the man, insolently, "be to insult her, then I suppose I'm guilty."

"It isn't so much that," returned the captain, with singular forbearance. He heard Mr. Conant growling like a dog by his side, and laid his hand upon him to quiet him.

"It might be that you couldn't help admiring the lady, who is as far above you as the main-truck is from the keelson, but you laid hands on her."

"Oh, pardon," cried François, "I did nothing of the sort."

"You lying dog!" roared Mr. Conant, stepping forward.

"Steady, Mr. Conant," said the captain. "The man's denial avails him nothing."

"Who says that I did anything?"

"I do," answered Susan.

"What did I?"

"You—you seized me in your arms and kissed me," answered the girl, red with shame and indignation at being forced to this confession in open day before the sneering men of the crew.

"Well, there's no harm in kissing a pretty girl —eh, mates?" insolently retorted François, turning to the crew, who greeted his insolent bravado with snickers of approbation.

And, indeed, for all her boy's clothes, Susan Hubbell made a picture most entrancing and attractive even to better men than the riff-raff forward.

"No harm, eh!" roared the captain. "We'll see about that. Four dozen lashes of the cat for you, and I'll disrate you."

"The man that lays his hand on me I kill," snarled François, grabbing his sheath-knife. "Me! the cat!"

"We'll see about that," said the captain. "Mr. Conant."

Mr. Conant needed no other word. Placing his hand on the rail, he vaulted to the deck, and before François knew what he was about the New Englander closed with him. The Frenchman was no match for the mate, and he realized it at once.

He struggled fiercely, however, to draw his knife, in the meanwhile appealing to the crew. They made a surge forward with evident intent to interfere, only to find the captain standing by the side of the two struggling figures, both pistols out.

"The first man that advances a step dies like a dog," said the captain. "I have two lives here."

"And I have two more here," cried Susan, at the same time handling her own weapons.

"You cowards!" screamed the struggling Frenchman, "let me get loose and I'll——"

"You won't get loose," said Mr. Conant grimly, "until we get ready to let you."

He had got a strangle hold on the man, and if he had not ceased to struggle would have broken his neck.

"I'll learn you," he muttered, "to insult a woman like Mistress Hubbell, there, you low, frog-eating French cur!"

The mate's language was not choice, but his meaning was unequivocal. He shook the Frenchman until the latter was almost black in the face. In fact, his sheath-knife, which he had managed to draw, was shaken from his hand and clattered to the deck. Mr. Conant kicked it out of the way, and then, at his request, Susan passing him a bit of line, he lashed the man's hands and held him perfectly helpless.

"Can you attend to him, Mr. Conant?" asked the captain, still holding the excited crew at bay.

"Certainly, sir." said the mate.

He dragged the hapless boatswain aft, lashed his hands to one of the stanchions supporting the rail of the poop-deck, entered the cabin, and came out with a cat-o'-nine-tails, a weapon with which ships' crews were very familiar in those days.

"All ready now, sir," he said to the captain.

Captain Hiram looked over the crew. His eye fell upon a Greek who, he had reason to believe, was one of the most disaffected.

"You, George," he cried, pointing his finger, "step up here."

The man came forward, cringing. The crew by this time were completely cowed.

"Take the cat and give him four dozen."

François, who was writhing and twisting against his lashing like a fish on the end of a line, swore horribly at the Greek.

"If you do—if you lay the weight of your hand on me—I'll cut your heart out when I'm free!"

"I daren't do it, sir," cried the Greek. "He'll do for me. You hear him."

"I hear him," said Mr. Conant, "and you can choose at once between being done for now by me or obeying your orders."

He thrust the cat into the trembling hand of the Greek.

"I can't help it, François," muttered the Greek, raising the cat.

"Hold on, there," said the mate; "he's not ready yet."

He stepped over toward the boatswain, took his shirt between his two hands, and tore it down from top to bottom, exposing his back.

"Now you can begin."

Susan walked aft, turning her back on the scene. She had seen men flogged before, always with horror, but never quite under circumstances like this.

The Greek raised the cat and struck the boatswain lightly over the shoulders.

"One!" said the mate; "and let me tell you, my friend, I don't generally demean myself by using the cat myself, but unless you put more force into it than that you'll get it on your own back."

There was something so threatening in the appearance of the big American that the

Greek struck this time with a hearty good will.

"Two!" said the mate, marking the red welts on the white flesh. "That's better," he nodded. "You'll get the swing of it pretty soon."

It was indeed so. The man did not love the boatswain, and something of the awful blood-lust that lies submerged in most hearts rose to the surface in the Greek and he found himself laying on the lash with determined vigor.

The boatswain took his punishment badly. He raved and swore and frothed and foamed like a madman, cursing every one on the ship. The woman, looking aft, tried to stop her ears from the hideous sounds. The mate counted imperturbably. By his side the Greek wielded the whip. The crew, cowed by the captain, remained forward.

Presently the punishment was over. The boatswain was unbound, handcuffs were slipped upon his wrists, and he was passed below into one of the spare cabins aft, where he was securely locked and left to think it over.

It was a rude, a cruel, a ruthless age, especially upon the sea, but there was some excuse for Captain Hiram. He had shipped the best men available; he had a precious daughter to protect and a most valuable ship to command.

He could not allow the slightest evidence of mutiny or insolence to go unchecked amid such a mass of men. He would show them that he was master, and would brook no interference from any one.

The fighting of the night before had been terrible enough for the woman, but this scene completely unnerved her. The boatswain's kiss had made her shudder with aversion, but his ravings and the sound of the beat of the whip had curdled the blood in her heart.

Captain Hiram dismissed the men, and they went forward or to their stations very silent and subdued. It was the first open clash that had come on the voyage, and he had undoubtedly shown himself the master. Composing his feelings as well as possible, he ascended the poopdeck and took a look at the enemy.

CHAPTER V

THE COMING OF THE BREEZE

THE outbreak of the boatswain and the evident sympathy of the crew rendered the position of the American ship doubly precarious. The men had fought well the first time. What would they do if they were called upon for another desperate defense? He questioned Mr. Conant, who had joined them, as to his opinion.

"Fight! Of course they'll fight," answered the mate, glooming over the situation. "Not because they love us or care a whipstitch for this ship, but because they don't want to choose between a British prison and a British ship. Some of them have been on English men-of-war and know what hells they are," continued the New Englander, who had the popular American idea of the time of the Revolution of the British ships, and which was, indeed, not without warrant.

The year was 1782, and the long war was

drawing to a close. The independence of the colonies was in sight, but that did not affect the status of the two ships in the least degree. One was as bent upon capture, and the other upon escape, as if the war had but just begun.

"Do you think they will attack us again if the breeze doesn't hold?" asked Susan.

"Hardly," returned her father.

"And they certainly wouldn't attack us during the day," continued the girl. "We should beat them off easily."

"What are they doing now?" interrupted the mate.

Susan turned and stared at the ship. The youngest and keenest-eyed, she made out distinctly what the others only saw dimly.

"They are getting boats overboard," she said.

"Certainly, not to move against us," exclaimed her father.

"They're going to tow, I think," said the mate.

"So they are," said Captain Hiram. "Susan, will you fetch me the glass?"

When she handed it to him he focused it on the bows of the other ship.

"Six boats full of men. I see no arms," he said. "Yes, they're for towing."

He shut to the glass with a snap.

"Get out the boats, Mr. Conant. We'll do
the same thing. There are four British prisoners who could pull an oar. Put them into a boat.
Yes, and bring up François, too, and let him go
with them. Do you take command of the boats
yourself, Mr. Conant."

"Aye, aye," returned the mate.

"But keep your weather-eye lifting. Don't
let the prisoners get away."

"They sha'n't escape me," returned the New
Englander, going forward.

Presently the four quarter-boats of the merchantman were swung overboard, each with its
crew reenforced by one of the British, who went
very unwillingly, coerced by the mate's threats
and the ugly looks of the Americans. In the
last boat, and pulling the stroke oar, right under
the mate's eye, where, as Mr. Conant said, he
could observe him and see that he didn't shirk,
sat François, a horrible object, more filled, if
possible, with rage and hate than before.

Towing is terrible work, and the small crew
of the *Hiram and Susan* were at a grave disadvantage in spite of the small size of their ship
as compared with the swarming numbers aboard
the frigate, which after several hours of heart-
breaking work was perceptibly nearer.

Relays of fresh men relieved those in the

frigate's boats, while the Americans had to keep on without any cessation, and well aware that when they gave out there would be none to take their places. Captain Hiram drove them to the very last limit. Presently human nature could do no more. Even the iron mate perceived the uselessness of further endeavors. He so told the captain, who leaned over the forecastle, staring ahead.

"Very well," said the latter; "drop the boats aft and send the men aboard."

Accordingly, the exhausted crew shipped their oars, swung the boats alongside, clambered on deck, and fell prostrated. Another tot of grog and a hearty dinner were served out, and an hour's rest allowed them.

The boatswain had come to the mast after the men had come on board, and had stood there, hat in hand, to speak to the captain.

"What is it?" said Captain Hubbell, observing him presently.

"If you please, Captain Hubbell," said the man submissively, "I want to beg your pardon and that of the young lady. I was mad. If you'll restore me to duty you'll find I'll act like a true man."

"I don't believe a word of it," said the captain grimly.

"Let him go to his duty, father," interrupted Susan, laying her hand upon his arm; "perhaps he is telling the truth."

"Not he," said the captain. "However, you can go forward and tell the men how it feels to cross my will, and if you offend again, by Heaven, I'll have you flogged till you drop dead."

"You are making a mistake, Miss Susan," said Mr. Conant. Not daring to approach the captain on the subject, he did so indirectly through Susan. "That's as black-hearted a villain as ever lived, and he means no good to you or to any one else. He'll corrupt the whole crew."

Susan looked doubtfully from the mate to her father.

"Oh, I don't know, Mr. Conant," said the captain. "He has been disgraced before them all, and I think he'll have little weight with them now. Besides, there'll be enmity between him and the Greek, and I look upon those two as the ringleaders in any possible trouble. Perhaps it's just as well to let him go."

"It is at least merciful," said Susan, whose heart had quivered at the frightful punishment inflicted upon the man. Her hatred and contempt and loathing of him were in nowise diminished, but certainly he had paid bitterly for his insult to her, and he stood before her a degraded, almost a broken, thing.

"Well," said the captain, "I guess we'll have to get the men into the boats again. Yon ship is perceptibly nearer, and——"

"I suppose so, sir," returned Mr. Conant, although he shrank from the task, knowing the temper of the men, most of whom had been awake the larger part of the night, and who had toiled under the hot sun until their backs had almost broken with the terrific strain of putting.

"Father," cried Susan, "look yonder." She pointed astern. "Isn't that a breeze? The water's ruffled."

"A catspaw," said the Captain.

"There's a promise of wind in the cloud yonder, sir," said the mate.

"We'll see. Keep fast the boats, Mr. Conant, and——"

One of the men on the deck below, leaning over the rail, saw the wind ruffling the surface of the water at that moment.

"Wind!" he shouted triumphantly, pointing.

"Aye, aye," returned the captain.

In another moment the sails gave a gentle flap different from the loose, purposeless slatting in the long roll in the sea.

"She feels it!" cried the captain. "Hands by the starboard braces!" He wetted his finger and held it up again. "It comes over the port quarter, I think. Brace in a bit. Hands aft to the wheel!"

"She gathers way!" cried Susan, staring over the side as the vessel began to slip gently through the blue water.

"So does the English ship," said the mate.

"We seem to have the better of it, though," commented Captain Hiram.

And, indeed, by a lucky chance the *Hiram and Susan* felt the full force of the wind some time before her pursuer.

"Mr. Conant," said the captain, keenly alive to the importance of neglecting no advantage, however temporary or slight, "clap tackles on all the sheets and halyards and get everything as flat as a board. Then send hands aloft with whips and buckets and wet everything down. We'll make the most of what we have. We're walking away from her as it is, and——"

His words were interrupted by a wild burst of cheering from the men, who could see the situation as well as he.

If they were afraid of Captain Hiram, they were doubly afraid of the British, and the orders of the captain, transmitted through the mate, were obeyed with a surprising alacrity that gave no indication of the mutinous spirit of a few hours before. In fact, the principal in the expressions of joy was the boastwain. He had got himself a clean shirt, and his torn back had been washed and swathed in bandages.

Save that he was deathly pale and his eyes glowed like coals, he presented but little change in his appearance.

The joy of the men on the *Hiram and Susan* was not for long, however, for presently the big frigate caught the force of the wind, and as she was a ship built not only to fight but to fly, it was soon demonstrated that she had the heels of the American. The difference in the rate of sailing, however, was so slight that it would be some time before the frigate would be within gunshot range.

Captain Hiram hoped to neutralize the superiority in sailing of the other ship by his knowledge of his own vessel and by his fine seamanship. He believed that he might hold on without being overhauled until nightfall, in which case, if the wind held, he might slip away in the darkness, deluding the enemy by false lights and whatsoever ruses would suggest themselves.

And, indeed, it seemed as if the long period of calm had been finally definitely broken, for the wind grew perceptibly stronger with every passing hour, and as the breeze strengthened the frigate diminished her distance from the trader. Like most ships of her class, the harder it blew the better she footed it, carrying sail easily when the merchantman would have to reduce her canvas or rip out her masts.

By nightfall it was blowing a good topgallant breeze, and the frigate was so close aboard that she had several times tried to reach the ship from one of her long main-deck guns. Fortunately, every shot fell appreciably short, and when the night closed down she had not yet made the required distance.

During the night Captain Hiram and Mr. Conant did everything in human power to shake off their pursuer. They lighted buoys and flung them overboard, and changed their course, the wind holding steady and blowing stronger all the time. Captain Hubbell carried a terrific spread of sail; the masts were bending and quivering, but he would take in nothing.

CHAPTER VI

BROADSIDE TO BROADSIDE

WHEN the day broke it showed to the anxious, naggard watchers the English frigate close at hand. Susan had remained on deck a large part of the night, but had finally gone below at her father's urgent insistence. When day dawned, although he was loath to awaken her, knowing how she must need sleep, her father summoned her to the deck. He did not know what might happen, and she was too valuable an adjunct to be neglected in the scheme of possible events.

"You sent for me, father?" said the young woman, as she slowly climbed the ladder to the raised poop.

"Yes, daughter."

"And for what reason?"

"To show you our friend off yonder," he replied, pointing to windward at the loom of the English ship, bright in the early sun.

Susan turned and stared at the frigate.

"The *Hiram and Susan* has in her more than a match," she said at last.

"Aye, yon ship has the heels of us, and look how she's weathered on us."

Susan nodded her head thoughtfully.

"She's well on our quarter now," she said.

"And quite within gunshot," added her wiser father. "Indeed, if she were to put her helm up——"

He stopped. The conclusion was too obvious to need description.

The mate here spoke.

"I wonder why they haven't opened fire yet?"

"What's the use of knocking up a prize already in their grasp?" returned the captain gloomily.

"I suppose you've tried them on every course, father?" asked Susan.

"Trust me for that."

"Well, then let me try," said the girl, unwilling to believe her eyes.

"If you like," said the captain, smiling a little, although he felt not at all inclined to merriment.

"The men—how do they behave?" she asked.

"Oh, well enough. They are a set of worthless lubbers."

"Perhaps I can inspire them," said the girl.

"Men," she called in a clear if somewhat high-pitched voice, "if yon frigate takes us it is fare-well to the ship and a British prison for all of you. We'll try once more to shake her off. Stand by to wear, and when I give the word jump as if your lives depended on it."

There was a hurried running to and fro of the heavy crew of the *Hiram and Susan*. A more villainous-looking set of men could hardly have been assembled. Only the offscourings of crea-tion had been available for the merchantman, and they looked it. The nondescripts on the *Hiram and Susan* would as lief have served un-der the British as under any other flag, other things being equal, and if capture had meant only a transfer of allegiance they would scarcely have raised a hand, save under compulsion, to prevent it.

But some of them were deserters from the British navy and had felt the rigors of its iron discipline; they knew that a short and summary justice would be meted out to them.

Others had no mind to exchange the rather free life of the merchant service, even though Captain Hiram ruled them with a necessarily heavy hand, for the horrors of Dartmoor or the British prison-ships. So they sprang to their stations with alacrity—an alacrity that would not have been manifested were the emergency less grave—at the command of a woman.

Lifting the glass from the hatch-cover, where the mate had laid it, Susan focused it on the frigate. Her quick eye discovered movement, apparently forward. Ah! they were casting loose one of the bow guns. Susan was not very familiar with the power of great guns, but she guessed that the frigate was in range, or nearly so, and that a long eighteen would probably send a shot over them or into them.

A single shot, if it struck aright, meant a crippled spar and a lost ship. If she intended to endeavor to save the *Hiram and Susan*, time for action had arrived. She shut to the telescope with a vicious snap, faced forward again, and without a trumpet, or even hollowing her hand, cried in her rich, clear voice:

"Stand by!"

At this peremptory signal the men, who under the direction of the mate had quickly arranged themselves at the sheets and braces, set taut upon or made ready to slack away the various ropes. The wheelsman steadied himself for the order which came sharp and clear.

"Up with the helm!

"Flatten in forward!

"Cast off the lee braces. Hands by the

weather fore and main and lee cross-jack braces. Mind the tacks and sheets.

"Brace in!

"Hard up with the helm!" she cried, leaning over the break of the poop, to the old sea-dog on the quarter-deck who whirled the wheel over spoke by spoke.

Then she turned and herself slacked off the spanker-sheet.

"Steady with the braces!" she cried as the great yards swung around.

"Now meet her with the helm. Aft, here, some of you, and brail in the spanker."

Her calculations had been made with the utmost accuracy, and the simple evolution had been performed with a despatch and precision which bespoke alike the skill of the commander and the responsiveness of the crew.

The two ships had been sailing side by side on the starboard tack. Now the *Hiram and Susan* was rushing broad away from the other at right angles to her former course, having been turned through an arc of ninety degrees. She was on her best point of sailing, before the wind, and was increasing the distance between her and the pursuer.

The frigate appeared to have been taken by surprise, for a perceptible interval elapsed be-

fore her helm was put up and by a similar evolution she swung after the merchant hooker.
This time, however, she was slightly to leeward.
She did not work quite so handily as the lighter
and smaller ship, it was evident, although when
it came to plain sailing the *Hiram and Susan* had
no advantage—indeed, was at a disadvantage.

"That was handsomely done, my girl," said
Captain Hubbell admiringly.

"Thank you, father," returned Susan in a
matter-of-fact tone, as if it were, as indeed it
was, a matter of course that she should do the
thing smartly and properly.

She shot another long look over the lee
quarter.

"We gained something on her by the move,
but we don't hold the advantage. See how she
walks up on us. I'll try her again on the wind."

" 'Tis useless," answered the captain; "I've
tried her half a dozen times during the night."

Again Susan's orders were carried out
smartly, and the *Hiram and Susan* was once
more brought to the wind on the starboard
tack.

Again the evolution was followed on the
frigate, and this time more smartly than before.
A careful scrunity did not convince Susan that
she had gained appreciably by the two maneu-

vers, and she rapidly came to the conclusion that with the two vessels on the same tack she presented a bigger target to the broadside of the frigate. Therefore, once more she threw her vessel before the wind, and once more the frigate followed her example. It was evident that the end was imminent and certain.

There was nothing to do in the way of seamanship to shake off the pursuer. Captain Hiram and his daughter stared a long time at the frigate. She was drawing nearer with every minute. Seamanship had failed, but there was still something to be done.

This time the captain took charge himself. A few rapid orders and the two ships were sailing side by side.

"What are you going to do, father?"

"I'm not going to give up yet," he said, "without a fight."

"What! Match this little merchant ship against yon frigate?" expostulated Mr. Conant, in astonishment.

"I am," said Captain Hiram firmly, "and you will oblige me by seeing my orders are carried out."

"Very good, sir," said the mate.

"Get the men to the guns. Go forward yourself on the forecastle and clear off the long-tom,

If we can manage to wing her perhaps we can shake her off."

"But, sir." Mr. Conant ventured further, "the minute we open fire she'll do the same, and——"

"You bandy words with my father!" cried Susan.

"Peace, my child," said Captain Hiram. "Mr. Conant is doing what he thinks is his duty, but I swear I'll not strike that flag yonder" —he pointed back to the Stars and Stripes— "without a fight for it, even if it sinks the ship."

"Think of your daughter, sir," said Mr. Conant.

"And I would rather go down with him than surrender," cried Susan.

Mr. Conant was as brave as a lion, but he was not foolhardy. To be sure, the ship did not belong to him, and he did not cherish for her that affection which Captain Hiram had. She had been the captain's home for these many years, and he loved her as he loved his native land.

The men heard with surprise the order to get to quarters and cast loose the guns. They had had their lesson, however, and, though reluctant, they obeyed.

Presently all was ready. The tarpaulins were

taken off the pivot-gun forward, and the gun, a long twelve-pounder, was loaded and primed. The six and four pounders in the broadside were useless at this range, but the long-tom could do some damage. At that date frigates only carried long eighteen-pounders, and not many of those, and while there were a score of long guns in the British frigate's broadside to overwhelm the one on the *Hiram and Susan*, most of the British guns were nines, and some were even sixes.

"Mr. Conant," bellowed the captain through his hand, "are you ready?"

"Yes, sir."

"Try to knock a mast out of her. Give your shot plenty of elevation and let her have it."

Mr. Conant himself knelt down and sighted the gun. With chocks and quoins he got the proper elevation, and then applied the loggerhead. There was a burst of smoke, a flash, a roar. A great rent appeared in the foretopsail of the frigate. The men on the *Hiram and Susan* yelled loudly.

"That's almost good enough," said the captain. "Another like that and she'll be minus a topmast."

"Load again, boys," said Mr. Conant, prudence deserting him at the success of his shot.

The men on the forecastle rapidly recharged the piece. Just as Mr. Conant knelt down to sight it there was a terriffic detonation. The whole side of the frigate burst into flame. She had let go her broadside full upon the *Hiram and Susan*.

The foretopmast went over the side with a crash. The men on the starboard training tackle on the forecastle were swept away as if they had been brushed aside with a broom. One shot buried itself under the hounds of the mainmast. Another smashed a quarter-boat and drove a crowd of splinters inward, one of which struck one of the Americans.

The English vessel forged ahead into the cloud of her own smoke, and a shift of the helm drove her down upon the *Hiram and Susan*.

"By God!" said Captain Hiram, "we'll not strike without striking back." He was in range now.

"Let her have it, men," he roared through his trumpet.

The small guns in the broadside of the merchantman barked out a sharp defiance. The range was point-blank, and some of the shot got home. Another smashing broadside came from the English frigate. Great holes were knocked in the bulwarks. Three of the guns were dismounted. A half-dozen men were hit. The main topsail-yard was shattered. Braces and ropes were cut, and the ship lay practically helpless.

Mad with rage, Captain Hiram jumped forward from the quarter-deck.

"Give it to him!" he roared. "Give it to the English dog! We'll sink rather than strike!"

But the men had no heart for further fighting, and, indeed, Captain Hiram's defiance was the act of a madman. The English ship had them close aboard, and another broadside would sink them.

A voice from the other ship came sharply to them out of the confusion.

"Do you strike?"

"No," roared Captain Hiram. "Give it to them, lads. Mr. Conant!"

But Mr. Conant lay on the deck, not dead, but knocked senseless by a splinter. The men at the broadside guns shrank away as Captain Hiram shouted at them.

"You're a fool!" yelled François, who had suddenly lost all of his submissiveness. "We'll be sunk alongside."

He threw down his linstock and turned away.

"Mutiny!" said the captain. "Get back to your quarters!"

He whipped out his pistol, pointed it full at the boatswain, and snapped it. There was a flash of the priming. The pistol hung fire.

"You will have it, will you?" cried François, turning upon him, knife in hand.

The captain struck at the boatswain with the but of the pistol, but the man was too quick for him.

François, turning upon him, buried his knife in the captain's heart.

Susan who saw it all, screamed wildly.

CHAPTER VII

THE RETICENT MATE

STANDING above on the poop, Susan's heart almost stopped beating; her scream died away unheeded in the confusion.

"Do you strike?" came down again from the frigate.

The smoke had blown away by this time, and she was close aboard. Mercifully her captain held his fire.

No response came from the American ship, and he could see that she was practically helpless.

The boatswain, after a defiant look at the dead captain, wiped his sheath-knife on his trousers, jumped lightly over the captain's body, and ran up the poop-ladder.

Susan thought he had come for her. She was too unnerved by the terrible catastrophe that had befallen her to think of resistance. She shrank back against the rail and looked at him, horrified. Her fingers fumbled at the pistol at her belt.

"I'll tend to you presently, my beauty," he cried, as he ran rapidly across the deck, cast off the halyards, and hauled down the United States flag from the gaff-end.

As it reached the deck he stamped his foot upon it.

"How dare you!" cried Susan, awakened to the insult in action.

She whipped out the pistol, but he ran to her, wrenched the weapon out of her hand, hurled it into the sea, and threw her wildly from him.

"I'm master of the ship now," he said in brutal triumph. "The captain's dead, killed by the enemy."

"You killed him," protested the girl. "I saw you."

"Nonsense!" was the rough reply.

"Where is Mr. Conant?" asked Susan.

"Dead on the forecastle."

Susan buried her face in her hands.

"Heave to!" cried a voice from the other ship.

"Aye, aye, sir," answered the boatswain. "As for you," he said, turning to Susan, "you'd better get below."

Without a word, Susan turned and entered the cabin.

"I'll send your father after you," said the man, as she left the deck.

But he was not to have things entirely his own way, for Mr. Conant at this juncture made his appearance in the waist. He had regained consciousness, and came aft, a little unsteady but apparently master of himself.

"What's this?" he said, as he stopped by the body of Captain Hiram.

"The captain was killed, sir," answered the boatswain smoothly, descending to the quarter-deck, "by the first broadside from the English frigate.

"Great God!" exclaimed Conant. "And Miss Hubbell?"

"She's below in her cabin, and unharmed, I think," returned the boatswain.

"Two of you carry the captain's body into the cabin," said the mate. "Who surrendered the ship?"

"I did, sir," answered the boatswain, fingering his knife.

He would have cut down the mate then and there had he dared, but there were too many witnesses, the deck was too quiet, and he was not yet sure of the crew.

"Very well," growled the New Englander. "Get forward, now, and get this raffle and wreck cleared away and secure the guns."

"Why don't you heave to?" came a peremptory voice down the wind from the frigate.

"Aye, aye," returned the mate, mounting the poop-ladder and giving the necessary orders.

And then, while the men busied themselves in a desultory fashion in securing the guns and clearing away the wreck, he leaned against the rail moodily and stared up toward the English ship.

"What ship is that?" came down the wind from the quarter of the English frigate, where a man stood balancing himself on the rail by holding to one of the backstays.

"The *Hiram and Susan,* of Boston," answered Conant sullenly through the trumpet. "What ship is that?" he roared in impertinent defiance.

"I'll send a boat aboard," was the reply. "And mind you stay as you are, if you don't want another dose."

Conant, who was a high-tempered young man, dashed the trumpet down on the deck in impotent rage.

From the English ship the shrilling of pipes came faintly across the intervening space. There was a hurried bustling on the deck. A heavy cutter filled with men dropped from the davits. She pulled to the starboard gangway. Two offi. cers stepped down the battens and took their places in the stern sheets. Handled to perfection, the boat got under way and rapidly pulled alongside.

The first who clambered through the gangway was a tall, slender, erect, authoritative-looking young man of perhaps five-and twenty, dressed in the blue-and-white British naval uniform, which he wore with easy grace and dignity. The single epaulet upon the shoulder indicated that he was a lieutenant in his majesty's service. He wore the usual sword, pistols, and cocked hat.

Hard on his heels came a bedirked youngster, a midshipman, evidently, and following them a dozen sea-dogs armed with cutlass and pistols.

Followed by the midshipman, the officer turned and walked aft, while the seamen spread themselves about the deck, in obedience to the quick directions of a boatswain's mate. Two went to the forecastle; the others occupied indicated stations, one old sea-dog relieving the man at the wheel.

The crew of the *Hiram and Susan,* for the

moment idle, hung over the rail, staring at the British ship.

Mr. Conant, from his position on the poop, made no move to welcome the officer, who with brisk steps and an air of great nanchalance, rapidly mounted the ladder.

"Are you the captain of this ship?" he began.

"No," blurted out the mate.

"Singularly courteous person," said the officer, with an abstracted air, as if addressing the atmosphere. "But perhaps my approach was too abrupt."

He took off his hat and bowed elaborately.

"Have I the honor," he began, with distinguished courtesy, "of addressing the master of the ship?"

"I told you once," growled the mate, who was both mystified and mocked the exaggerated politeness of the other, "that I was not."

"Will you pardon my excessive stupidity and in turn kindly inform me who and what you are?"

"None of your business!" roared the mate, who had the Yankee hatred of the English fully developed.

"Indeed! Mr. Merryfield"—this to the midshipman, who had stood by impatiently enough during the interview—"will you kindly ask the boatswain's mate to send Johnson and Palmer —I believe they are the two stoutest men in the crew—up on the poop?"

The midshipman was only too glad to transmit the order, to which the two seamen, who had heard all, responded with alacrity. The performance had been very tame, so far, and they were hoping that Providence would be kind to them and that the mate's ill temper might continue.

"Perhaps," said the officer, pointing to Conant, "these worthy seamen may assist you to answer my courteous questions with proper civility. If you do not, although it will be painful to me and to you also, I shall have to order you taken to the fo'c's'l."

An angry snarl was the only reply.

Meanwhile, Messrs. Palmer and Johnson, two of the burliest tars that ever trod a ship's deck, ranged themselves alongside of the mate. At a nod from the officer Johnson drew and cocked his pistol.

"Now, sir," began the former, "you perceive the seriousness of your situation. Who and what are you?"

"I'm the mate of this ship," returned the New Englander, who realized the futility and folly of his previous course.

"What is your name?"

"Conant."

"Oh, Mr. Conant, charmed to make your acquaintance, although the circumstances are not altogether favorable for unrestrained social intercourse."

"Ask me what you want to know and lemme go," stammered out the mate, furiously angry at this badinage.

"In good time, my dear sir. My time, that is. What is the name of the ship?"

"The *Hiram and Susan*."

"Good Lord! Where from, and whither bound?"

"From Bordeaux to Boston."

"And what is your cargo?"

"It's in the manifest, below in the captain's cabin."

"But I am here, my good sir."

"Damnation!" growled the mate.

"A poor lading, and one that is apt to bring you to hell, sir," commented the officer, with annoying gravity.

"Silks and wines and jimcracks and wimmen's fixin's," said Mr. Conant desperately.

"Ah 'tis almost as dangerous a cargo," was the reply of the Englishman, who seemed to have a pretty wit, though the mate found him not at all humorous.

The seaman, who had heard with great enjoyment everything that had gone, broke into a cheer—over the liquid lading, not the humor of their officer.

"Very good—very good," continued the young man, smiling at the enthusiasm of his men; and, indeed, he himself was enjoying the situation greatly. "And you said you were the mate. Where is the captain?"

"Dead. Killed by your first broadside."

"What was his name?"

"Hiram Hubbell."

"How quaint!" said the officer. "Such a name ought almost to make him willing to die. And Susan?"

"His wife."

"Is she——"

"Dead, too," said the mate.

"Well, you made a fine fight for your ship," said the officer. "It went hard with that boarding party night before last. That was handsomely done, but you were foolish this morning."

"That's not my business," said the mate gruffly. "Captain Hubbell gave the orders. It was his ship."

"I see. Well, we won't blame him now that he's dead, but what he could have thought of in attempting to engage at pistol-shot distance with a frigate like ours I can't see. Our captain is hot enough about it, wasting four days and a score of men on a ship like this."

"You needn't have wasted a minute on us if you hadn't wanted to," said the mate grimly.

"That'll do," returned the officer shortly. "Palmer, you may go. Johnson also. Now, sir, you are a prize to his Britannic majesty's ship *Rockingham*, forty-four. I shall leave Mr. Merryfield here temporarily in charge. You will find him a gentleman of refined courtesy, but of great spirit and enterprise, with whom it would not be well to trifle.

"And let me assure you"—his voice lost its banter and he spoke curtly—"the slightest discourtesy or rebellion will be met by severe punishment later. For the present, Mr. Merryfield, you will see that the crew of the *Hiram and Susan* remain on deck, and that this gentleman be not allowed to go below. You will be relieved in good time. Meanwhile, set the men to work clearing up the deck."

"Very good, sir," answered the midshipman importantly, at the same time elaborately drawing and cocking his pistol, while he took his position on the lee rail, whence he could cover the unarmed mate and keep watch upon the deck.

CHAPTER VIII

THE YOUTH IN THE CABIN

IN half an hour or so the same boarding officer came back to the prize. A large and a small
sea-chest were swung aboard, and a dozen sailors' bags, after which the cutter returned to the
frigate with the British wounded and prisoners
of the night before.

Without taking any notice of the mate, the
young lieutenant ran up on the poop, nodded to
Mr. Merryfield, ordered the yards swung, and
filled away. One of the seamen, by his direction, hoisted the British flag, and with the echo
of three cheers from the frigate, which whirled
about on her heel and went broad off on her
course, the two vessels started away from each
other.

The men went to work to repair damages
with a will, and by means of a spare topmast
they soon had the merchantman in fair condition.

The *Hiram and Susan* had another master

and another port of destination. For the first time in the past six years, the English ensign— which, by the way, was the flag under which she had been launched—rippled out from the gaff-end. Conditions had changed, however, since the launching of the *Hiram and Susan,* and how Captain Hiram, lying cold and still in the cabin, would have writhed with shame and mortification could he have known about it!

Having sent the prisoners forward into the forepeak, with the exception of the mate, who was left undisturbed for the present, the lieutenant set the watch, gave Mr. Merryfield the course and sailing directions, and went below to the cabin for an examination of the ship's papers.

Mr. Conant had curtly declined to accompany him.

The lieutenant entered the cabin alone. He was in no way prepared for what he saw when he opened the door. Lying on the transom, on the starboard side of the cuddy, was the body of the captain. He stood at gaze a moment, and then stepped over to the transom and looked at the face of the dead. Conqueror and conquered, face to face.

It was a stern, grim, powerful face—set in the iron repose of death—that met his gaze.

The artificial expression, lent to humanity by the exercise of the human will had gone, and naked to his search the man lay stark and still before him. If the spirit of Captain Hiram hovered about the cabin he had so long tenanted, he had no cause for shame at the revelation of dissolution, for it was a brave, manly, resolute aspect he presented, and withal there were lines of tenderness about the mouth and lips which did not bespeak weakness, and which not even the finger of the death-angel had eradicated.

There was something so somberly tragic in the dead man lying there, having lost his life and ship coincidently, that the young man, to whom the sight of death was not unfamiliar, stood long in silent contemplation. He could recognize good qualities even in an enemy, and he saw them there and gave them the honest man's meed of appreciation.

"A good man and a true," he murmured at last. "Brave, honest, and intelligent, if I can read a man's soul in his look. A worthy master of a fine ship."

Although still young, he was already an accomplished sailor, and had previously noted the fine lines of the *Hiram and Susan* during the chase and since he had been aboard her.

"This evidently is the *Hiram*," he continued

thoughtfully. "Well, sir, we shall send you overboard presently in a proper seamanlike way, with the prayers of the Church and our sympathetic farewell. Hiram! What queer names these Yankees have. I wonder what Susan was like and who was she."

He stepped to the door opening in the break of the poop upon the quarter-deck and spoke to a seaman standing in the waist. Presently the voice of the boatswain's mate rolled along the deck calling Palmer to report to the cabin with a sailmaker's needle, and in a moment later that veteran made a sea-scrape before the officer.

"Palmer," began the lieutenant, "this"— pointing to the prostrate figure on the transom —"is—was—the master of the ship. You will get a hammock and sew him up in it, and then we'll take him on deck. Get the other dead in shape also. Summon the men, including the Yankee crew, and we'll put their dead overboard in seamanlike fashion."

"Aye, aye, sir," returned the seaman, stepping over toward the transom.

"Wait!" said a clear voice at the moment, and there stepped into the rather dimly lighted cabin a tall, slight, and boyish-looking figure, clad in the seaman's ordinary garb, with loose, flowing trousers at the knee and woolen stockings and buckled shoes, with blouse open at the throat and sailor jacket around the shoulders— a pale-faced, gold-crowned figure.

The newcomer stood swaying uncertainly in the doorway with the uneasy motion of the ship. The eyes of the young person sought vaguely those of the lieutenant, turned toward the seaman who had stopped by the transom, and then, with a low cry, Susan ran swiftly across the deck, knelt down, and took the head of Captain Hiram in her arms and laid her own head upon his broad breast and burst into a passion of weeping.

"No, no—I can't let him go! Don't take him away from me! Father! Father!"

The hat of the young officer came off at once. He stood uncertainly for a few moments, and then stepped across the cabin and laid his hand gently on the shoulder of the prostrate figure.

"My lad," he said gently, with no trace of gay carelessness in his voice now, "was it indeed your father?"

A nod of the head was the answer.

"Poor boy!" came from the lieutenant. "And he died when?"

"He was murdered this morning."

The lieutenant did not take this charge literally. He supposed it arose from the excitement in the speaker's mind, and that the captain had been killed in the battle.

Susan divined the officer's mistake. She spoke instantly and vehemently.

"I mean what I say."

"But I thought he was killed by a shot from our ship."

"No. One of his own crew struck him down."

"Impossible!"

"I saw it with my own eyes."

"But why?"

"He was mutinous, and insulting to me, and my father had him flogged. Later he was restored to duty at my intercession, and in the excitement of this morning's battle he stabbed his captain."

The lieutenant stared amazed at this tragic revelation. It appeared to him so improbable that he fancied the young man must be distraught.

"See!" cried Susan, stepping nearer to her father and throwing open his coat and waistcoat. "There!"

The lieutenant bent over, and in the breast of the dead man could be seen the long, clean knife-thrust, cut through the shirt and pointed straight for the heart.

"No bullet or splinter did that," he remarked gravely.

"It is true, you see."

"It would seem so.   What is the name of the man?"

"François, our bo's'n."

"I shall deal with him presently."

"You will hang him to the yard-arm for murder?"

"Not without a trial, young man."

"But he is guilty."

"This is England now," returned the officer. "He must be tried.   I have no power to do more than prefer charges, but with your testimony and mine as to this wound, and perhaps some of the other men may have seen it, there will be no doubt but that justice will be done.   Meanwhile, I will have him put in irons."

"You will get no help from the other members of the crew.   They are about ready to mutiny now," returned Susan incautiously.

"I see," said the lieutenant.   "Well, I shall take due precautions.   Meanwhile, your father should be—— We must bury him this morning, I think, with the others of your men."

"Yes, yes, I know," returned the other.   "It must be, and he would rather be cast into the sea that he has loved than be buried on the shore."

"Certainly, I understand that," said the lieutenant, "and if you have no objection, it shall be this morning."

Now, there was something in the sight of that kneeling figure that affected him strangely. He had never seen a boy who so powerfully appealed to him.

"Yes," was the answer. "Now as well as any time."

"You would not like to read the service yourself, I suppose?"

"I could not," said the other, rising.

"Your mate?"

"I don't know. I'm afraid that he——"

"I shall be glad to do it myself. Death wipes out all enmities, and your father and I and all true men are friends now."

"Thank you," was the reply; "if you will."

"Very well, then."

At this moment Palmer and one of his mates came into the cabin, bringing a hammock. Susan pressed a long kiss upon the cold lips of the old man, drew herself once more upon her feet, and with a long look of farewell of him turned away.

It took but a short time for the sail-maker's

mate and his assistant to prepare the body for burial. Summoned by Palmer, a couple of seamen lifted the body and carried it out on deck. The two in the cabin heard the boatswain's pipe again shrilling, and his deep cry, "All hands bury the dead," came mournfully into the little room.

"My prayer-book is in my sea-chest, and it has not been opened," said the young officer.

"You may have mine," said the girl, turning into the stateroom and coming back with it.

"Thank you. Now I shall go on deck and see that everything is made ready—— You wish to stay here, or——"

"I want to be there," came the quick reply.

"Very well; I'll send Mr. Merryfield for you."

"Men," said the lieutenant, when he reached the quarter-deck, "we're going to commit to the deep the bodies of the American captain and of the sailors who were killed in the fight. Bring the Yankee crew upon deck. Guard them closely."

"You, sir"—to Mr. Conant—"will stand with Mr. Merryfield and myself, and if you will be kind enough to fetch the American flag you just struck, which you'll find in the signal-chest, we will throw it over the captain, and you can draw it aside, if you will, at the proper moment."

"Who is going to read the service?"

"I am, at the request of the dead man's son."

"Son!" exclaimed the mate, and then stopped open-mouthed, evidently in doubt whether to say more or not.

But the officer paid no attention to him whatsoever.

The practised seamen rigged gratings at the lee gangway—the starboard one in this instance —and laid the bodies upon them. The mate covered the captain's body with the American flag—captain and sailors, master and men, side by side, all earthly distinctions abolished by the greatest of levelers, death.

The American crew—American in name only —were called from below and placed forward of the gratings, surrounded by an English guard, heavily armed. At a word from the lieutenant Mr. Merryfield went to the cabin and returned, followed by the daughter of the captain. She took her place just back of the lieutenant, who considerately refrained from glancing at her.

The English officer began the beautiful service in a sympathetic, carefully modulated voice. It was rather a pitiful end for Captain Hiram, this being buried by an alien, a stranger, and an enemy, but perhaps he recked little of it fronting the great sum-total of the future.

At the proper time the men who bore the inboard ends of the gratings tilted them. There was another flash like that which had occurred from the same spot on the same ship twenty years before, and Captain Hiram's body had gone into the same great deep which had received into its cool embrace the body of his young wife."

CHAPTER IX

SOMETIMES THE LAW IS IRKSOME

"PIPE down. Send the prisoners below," quietly said the lieutenant as the final word died away.

And then he turned to confront the shaking figure behind him. Admirable had been Susan's control until that final moment when the body of Captain Hiram fell away, and then a low sob rose mournfully above the singing of the wind through the rigging, the rolling and splash of the ship plowing athwart the seas.

As the lieutenant's eyes fell upon her in the full light of broad day he saw at once that she was a woman. The prayer-book dropped from his fingers, and he stared in surprise, amazement, and admiration. The loose-fitting garments could not disguise the elegance of the figure any more than the male habiliments could hide the sex of the wearer.

"I thought," he began falteringly, "you said you were the captain's son."

"His daughter," returned Susan, and for the first time, perhaps, in her life, she became conscious of the fact that she was not wearing the garments of her sex, before the curious, surprised, admiring, yet entirely respectful glance of the young man.

A slow color flushed her face. She put her hands up to her cheeks and across her eyes, and then turned and went swiftly into the cabin, leaving the officer staring after her in puzzled bewilderment.

Mr. Conant's rather harsh laugh broke the embarrassed pause.

"You don't seem equal to the sight of a woman," he began.

"Not in that guise, certainly," returned the other. "Does she always dress in that way?"

"Generally at sea," answered the mate. "I've been with Cap'n Hiram three or four years now, and——"

"And you got used to it, I suppose?"

"Jes' so. On shore she rigs herself out in proper female clothes, but here she dresses like the rest of us."

"The practice has its advantages, I presume," returned the officer.

"It has. You see, she sometimes goes aloft,

and sometimes she takes an oar, and sometimes she takes the deck."

"Takes the deck?"

"That's what I said. She's as good a seaman as I am, or anybody. It was her that handled the ship this morning."

"What! You don't mean——"

"I do indeed, jes' that, and you'll allow, I guess, that she did it well."

"Brilliantly," returned the officer. "I had given the captain credit for that, Mr. Mate. We were all surprised, and I may say delighted, at the skill and smartness shown."

"He had nothin' to do with it. She was in command. Him and her owned the ship, and she often handled it, him permitting. He didn't generally balk her in anything she wanted. She usually gets her own way."

"Naturally. And you say she owns half the ship?"

"She owns it all now. It came to her through her mother."

"And what is her name, may I ask?"

The mate was unusually communicative, for some reason of his own, and he answered readily questions that a few hours before he had refused to discuss."

"Her name's Susan."

"The *Hiram and Susan?*"

"Exac'ly. Susan Hubbell—Miss Susan Hubbell. And I may say that it's probable she and I'll get together and make a match of it. You see, she's got no one but me now."

"Indeed," said the lieutenant, "if that be the case——" and there was an emphasis on the "if" which the mate did not fail to note—"you'll be a very lucky fellow."

"I guess so," returned the other. " 'Tain't exactly settled, but——"

"Well, we'll leave the discussion of that for a later time. In the meantime, will you give me your parole, if I allow you to occupy the cabin and give you the run of the after part of the ship, that you will make no effort to recapture the ship?"

"See you damned first!" said the mate.

"Very good," replied the other, smiling. "I like your frankness, even if it isn't accompanied by the courtesy which should obtain even between a prisoner and captor. I trust I shall not forget to be a gentleman, however I may be encouraged thereto by your bad example."

In this manner the English officer always got on the mate's nerves.

"Well, you don't expect me to throw away any chance of gettin' back my ship, do you?"

"Miss Susan Hubbell's ship."

"Well, what's hers is goin' to be mine, and, anyway, I'm goin' to get free if I can."

"I ought to put you in double irons," said the young man suavely, "after such a declaration, but I think it will hardly be necessary. I can either lock you in your cabin or send you below with your men."

"Please yourself about that," said the mate sturdily.

"Below with the men it is, then. Understand, of course, that the minute you'll give me your parole your condition will change."

"You've made that clear enough. I give no paroles."

"Very good, sir."

Before the rest of the men followed the mate forward and below the Englishman caused François, the boatswain, to be put in double irons. Mr. Conant naturally demanded the meaning of this performance, quick to resent such an indignity toward one of his men, even though he loathed and despised him. And to him the English officer vouchsafed a brief explanation.

"He is accused of murder," he said, "by the captain's daughter. She declares she saw him stab his captain when we were exchanging broadsides."

"It's a lie!" exclaimed the boatswain promptly.

"What!" roared the mate.

"It's a lie," persisted François, confident that since the burial of the body no one could contradict him by pointing to the wound. "He was struck by a splinter."

"Not so," answered the lieutenant coolly, "for I myself saw the wound from which he died—a knife-thrust in the heart."

The mate rushed at the helpless boatswain, and perhaps would have thrown him overboard in his fury had not the English seamen, by direction of their officer, quickly interposed.

"Mr. Conant," said the latter promptly, "you will oblige me by keeping your hands off that man. When we reach England he shall be tried for murder, and I have no doubt he will be hanged, as he deserves. Did any of you other men see the blow?"

Many of them had, but they answered not a word. In one sense the boatswain, by braving the lieutenant, unified their antagonism to England, which was even greater than their hatred of the mate.

"You will give me your word about this, sir,"

continued the lieutenant, "although you refused it in the other case."

"Word for what?" asked the New Englander.

"That you will refrain from doing him any harm, and that you will keep him well guarded."

"I'll keep him well guarded," was the bitter answer.

"And your hands off of him?"

"Oh, very well," assented the mate reluctantly, for even he could see that the orderly course of the law was the best; "I give you my word. I'll do him no harm. You've no objection to bread and water for him, though, have you?"

"None whatever," answered the lieutenant. "But, remember, hands off."

"I'll remember. Have you heard what caused the whole trouble?"

"I have heard something about it. He was mutinous, and was flogged, and out of revenge——"

"That's not quite all," returned Mr. Conant. "He offered a deadly insult to the captain's daughter. It was her who repulsed your boat-attack over the stern, and in the darkness this hound ran up on the poop, seized her unsuspectin', kissed her, and said he loved her." The mate spat violently over the side as indication of his deep disgust.

"Do you know, Mr. Conant," said the lieutenant quietly—he was a very quiet young man, as a rule—"I am almost sorry that you gave me your word to keep your hands off of him."

"I can take it back if you want me to," returned the other promptly.

"No," said the lieutenant. "The law must deal with him, but I sometimes find the law a very irksome thing."

The boatswain opened his mouth to speak.

The lieutenant turned on him in fury.

"Not a word!" he roared, with a sudden burst of passion. "If I consulted my inclination you would be swinging from that yardarm. I am saving your life, and it behooves you to be silent. Go forward all, now. Good morning, Mr. Conant, a pleasant voyage to you, and may you find the society of the forehold agreeable."

Somehow, the rough, ill-tempered mate had got on the edge of the English officer's nerves in turn, for all his polite way of dealing with him, and he was glad to see him go forward. Indeed, he would not have offered him a choice of places of confinement, but would have had him locked in his cabin, had it not been for Miss Susan Hubbell.

The Englishman had a great desire to see more of that young lady, and he realized that the presence of another man behind a thin bulk-head would effectually bar any confidences or other conversation, and put a damper upon an acquaintance which bade fair to relieve the te-dium of what would probably be an otherwise eventless voyage to England.

And the more he thought of it the less he liked the idea of any future relationship what-soever between Mr. Owen Conant and Miss Susan Hubbell. It went distinctly against his sense of the universal fitness of things that a woman so beautiful, and so accomplished in so strange a way, should be wasted upon such a sea-dog—gruff, unmannerly, and uncouth—as the mate.

He had met and been thrown in the society of women of the highest social station all his life, but he had never seen any one of precisely the characteristics of this American girl, and he was eager to know more of her. With that end in view, he turned presently, after observing the course and speaking a word or two with his young subordinate, and re-entered the cabin.

CHAPTER X

ONCE! TWICE! THRICE!

THE cabin, of course, was empty. The lieutenant had as yet enjoyed no opportunity for inspecting it, and now that he had the chance he hesitated. He would not have stood upon ceremony a moment had the conditions been other than they were. He would have made direct for the captain's stateroom, and afterward have examined the others.

But the presence on the ship of the captain's daughter complicated matters. She might be in her dead father's cabin, or she might be in some other, and after the experience of a few moments ago he hesitated about intruding upon her grief, wherever she might be. Yet it was clearly necessary for him to examine the ship's papers, and if it had not been, the desire that possessed him for a further acquaintance with the young woman who had so charmingly masqueraded in men's clothes would have urged him to action.

By way of preliminary, he coughed once, and again more loudly. So far as he could observe, there was no response. Possibly he had not been heard above the natural noises of the straining ship in the high seas.

Grown desperate, he stepped toward the door of the captain's cabin, or at least what in ships of that class was usually the captain's cabin, and tapped lightly upon it. After waiting a moment for a response and receiving none, he opened it, only to be confronted by a very surprised and angry woman in some disarray of clothing. He had time to mark, however, that it was feminine clothing, if of a very plain and simple fashion, when a high and indignant voice cut athwart his amazement.

"Are prisoners allowed no privacy, sir, on your ship?"

"I beg your pardon," began the lieutenant, staring in bewildered appreciation of the loveliness before him, "but——"

"Will you close the door?" cried the girl, with a stamp of her foot, the color flaming into her face again. It was the second time he had made her blush; once when she wore the dress of the other sex, and this time in that of her own.

He turned precipitately, dragging the door

after him, and then found himself just where he had been before—alone in the cabin. He was making no progress, unless it was to get into the bad graces of the young lady, whom he found charming in any guise, and of whom he could say that the more frequently he saw her the more frequently he desired to be in her company.

He stood baffled yet amused by the situation, and then he knocked again on the cabin door, this time more firmly.

"Am I not to be allowed to dress in peace?" came from the other side of the door with asperity.

"Certainly, madam; by all means. But will you allow me—may I be permitted to——"

"Well, what is it?"

"I wish to see you out here as soon as you are ready to receive me," returned the abashed lieutenant.

"If you will let me alone I shall be ready in a few moments," came back the answer viciously through the door.

Those moments were long ones to the young man idling on the transom and staring at the after-cabin bulkhead.

Now, Susan Hubbell was as little given to the adornment of her person as any woman,

for she had associated with men none of whom
could she by any possibility regard as equals, or
companions, or individuals whose admiration
she cared to excite, or whose attention she
wished to provoke. For all the vaporings of the
mate, she regarded him from very much the
point of view that the average shipmaster regarded his principal subordinate in those days,
and any closer alliance, which, the wish being
father to the thought, he had alluded to, had
never entered her head.

She had worn the clothes of the sailor lad
with a careless indifference which was in keeping with the assumption of the youthful and
masculine station. Of course, she was naturally
fond of pretty things, but she was that *rara avis*
in any age, a woman who knew little and cared
less about the fashions. Her feminine and
proper garments were cut for comfort and con-
venience.

Beautiful she would ever be, perhaps more
beautiful in the unadorned simplicity of the garments of her fancy than in the more elaborate
toilets of a day in which dress played, if possible, a larger part in feminine economy—and in
masculine extravagance—than it does even at
present. There was a wild picturesqueness
about her attire, a combination of color and

form accentuating her freedom, which was as novel and as refreshing as the variant moods and colors of the ocean which had been her home. In a word, she might not be fashionable, but she was never dowdy.

Association with her plain but honest and high-souled father had taught her instinctively to recognize a gentleman, and for practically the first time in her life she had been thrown in contact with one who fully deserved that title. Likewise for the first time she found herself thinking seriously of the things that she was putting on.

The mirror was an object of little use in her sea boudoir, but to-day she stared longer and harder into it than she had ever done in her life. In her infrequent visits to great cities while the *Hiram and Susan* was receiving its lading in some adjacent port, she had seen women of fashion, or at least persons she supposed might come in that category, and the curious nature of the dresses they wore had moved her amusement and contempt until to-day.

Yet in the matter of expense, no money had been spared to fit out My Lady Susan in the sweetest way. In cut, in shape, in style, her clothes might have a simplicity which marked her own individuality, but in material there was nothing better. Captain Hiram had not traded with France for many years, bringing silks and furbelows to America, without knowing the value of the things he carried.

The more she surveyed herself the more she wished that she was not differentiated by whatsoever cause from the rest of her sisters. There is some virtue in monotony after all. To be like the others is sometimes salvation to a disquieted soul.

Susan, however, had to make the best of a bad beginning. Even her stubbornly curly hair, which she wore manlike, tied in a club behind, could not be made to change its character on so short a notice. There was no help for it. She had to go out in what she had. Shamefacedly at last, therefore, she opened the door and stepped into the cabin.

And then, with a rush of recollection, she realized that for a whole half hour she had forgotten her father.

The familiar room, the officer sitting on the transom where her father used to sit, brought it all back to her, and the memory came with an added poignancy because she recognized the fact that a chance meeting with the veriest stranger had temporarily driven grief from her heart. She went pale again before his glance and then her eyes filled with tears.

"Don't cry," he said sympathetically, rising and offering his hand. "You must be brave, and——"

His words recalled her to herself.

"I shall not give way again," she answered. "And before anything else, I want to thank you for your kindness in having read the service for my father. I do truly appreciate it, and I am deeply grateful."

"Pray say no more, my dear madam"—the unfamiliar word startled her a little—"I am glad to be of any service to you whatsoever."

"It was foolish of me to run away as I did, but, you see, you startled me, and——"

"Indeed, I protest, ma'am, it was most natural for you."

He intended to reassure her. But she put another contsruction upon his remark—that he was pointedly alluding to her masculine dress. She was quick in temper and sudden and hasty in action. Her face flamed again and her eyes sparkled.

"I'm not ashamed of it at all, I beg to assure you," she retorted fiercely.

"Not ashamed? I don't understand!"

"Well, you would if you knew me better. I

wear it generally on the sea. I feel so much more free, and——"

"Are you referring to your dress?"

"Certainly; didn't you mean that?"

"Of course not, but since you mention it, I'm sure it's most becoming—and appropriate as well."

"How dare you refer to it in the slightest degree?" began Susan perversely.

"Well, ma'am, I am indeed unfortunate. I seem to do nothing but annoy you," returned the young man, biting his lip to suppress his amusement. "I thought it was you that brought the subject up, and I merely wanted to reassure you."

"I want none of your assurances, sir. I want to know what you are going to do with me and my ship, and with the murderer of my father?"

That was a question which from one point of view it was not easy to answer.

Manlike, he took the line of least resistance.

"The murderer I have put in double irons; your mate is looking after him. Your ship, I regret to say, is prize to his Britannic majesty's ship *Rockingham,* of which I am, or was, the third lieutenant. I have been ordered to carry her into Portsmouth, where the boatswain will be tried, and of course I have no option but to obey my orders."

"And what will become of the ship then?"

"I—I suppose it will be condemned and sold, and——"

"How I hate the English!" cried the girl. "They forced this war upon us and now they take our property and sink our ships."

"Quite so," said the young man coolly, "but if my memory serves me, your own ships have been doing some of the sinking and taking. I was a midshipman on the *Drake* when she struck to the *Ranger*, and I have the mark of an American bullet on me yet."

"I wish," snapped out the girl impulsively, that it had——"

"Ah, yes," interrupted the young man, "but you see it did not, and if it had I should not have had the pleasure of this *tête-à-tête* with you."

"How can you talk so lightly of it," she said reproachfully, "when it means the loss of my ship just as I had lost my father."

"Forgive me," pleaded the young man in deep contrition. "I shouldn't have said that; but if the Yankee bullet had gone an inch nearer my heart, so that I could not be here, there might have been some one else who would, who might——"

"Who might not have shown me your distinguished consideration?"

"Well, I don't like to put it that way, but that was the substance of my thought."

"Then you intend to show me consideration?"

"The highest I have at command, believe me."

"And as a beginning, you may enter my private cabin where I am dressing, without knocking."

"Now, there you do me an injustice, for I both coughed and knocked."

"You should have waited for my permission, sir. I was just deliberating after you knocked."

"I really can do little except again to apologize. You see, the masters of merchant ships usually occupy that starboard cabin, and I naturally supposed that it was empty, since your father——"

"He gave it to me ever since I was old enough to have a cabin by myself. He used to call me the little master of the ship." Her voice faltered. "He was so good to me," she went on unrestrainedly.

"I'm sure of it. He looked good and honest and true."

"Thank you for that," she answered, ready to have forgiven him almost everything for those simple, spontaneous words.

A little pause fell between them, which, in spite of his readiness, he hardly knew how to break.

It was she who spoke first.

"You've told me what is to be done with my ship. Now, what will become of me?"

This was the puzzling part of the question which he would fain have evaded, but there was no escape from the direct interrogation now.

"My dear young lady," he began, "I hardly know what to say. If I had a mother, or a sister, or any near female relative, I should use my influence with the Admiralty to have you paroled in the care of one of them, but I am practically alone in the world."

"Like myself," commented the girl pathetically.

"Like yourself. That makes me the more wishful to befriend you," he went on with the deep gravity befitting such serious conversation. "In short, I cannot say just now what shall be your fate, but, you may depend upon me, I shall do the best I can do for you. We shall have time to consider what to do before we reach

Portsmouth, although this ship seems a good goer."

"There are very few on the ocean that have the heels of her."

"I believe that. The *Rockingham* is our newest frigate. She is built on a French model, too, else we shouldn't have overhauled you."

"We've escaped from many of your ships before."

"Yes, you Americans certainly know how to lay down swift keels."

"And to fight them, too," she burst out impulsively.

"Aye, that also. Indeed, I may say to you that I deplore this war, and I wish to God that we could have arranged our differences amicably."

"You might have done so," returned the girl, "if you had not tried to tax us to death, and——"

"We, at least," interrupted the young man gently but inflexibly, "will not fail to be good friends while I have charge of the ship."

"I hope not," she answered slowly, unable, however unwilling, to withstand such winning courtesy and consideration.

"Now, you understand, of course, that you have the entire freedom of the vessel. If you will give me your father's public papers, you shall take charge of everything else that belongs to him. The inviolability of your cabin shall be respected by Mr. Merryfield and myself, who are the only persons who will enter here, if I have to put a sentry before the door."

"Your word, sir, will protect me as well as an armed man," she retorted with one of those swift changes in manner peculiar to her and in which much of her fascination lay.

"I thank you, and if you have a wish you have only to express it. Now, with your permission, I will look over the papers, the ship's papers, and then, as it is long past eight bells, I shall have dinner served here, and perhaps you will allow me the privilege of dining with you."

"The ship is yours. Why should I be consulted?" returned the girl bitterly.

"Nay, madam, until I have turned her over to the authorities at Portsmouth, 'tis yours, and save in the matter of laying course, I beg you so to regard her as your own still."

"You are very kind," said the girl, "but you cannot alter the fact that you are master and I am your prisoner."

She dropped her head on her hands where she sat leaning over the cabin table and slow tears trickled down her fingers. The young man thought that if affairs continued as they tended, in one very definite sense he would be the girl's prisoner and she would be the captor before the voyage was ended.

"Don't cry," he said at last, "you promised to be brave, you know, and you Americans have a reputation for courage which you must sustain."

It was a wise appeal. She dashed the tears from her face with the back of her hand and looked up at him, the ghost of a smile flickering upon her lips. And she was one of the very few women who look pretty when they cry, he noted.

"You are right," she said, "I'll not do it again. Now I will go and get the papers, but before I do, won't you tell me your name?"

"My name is"—he hesitated a moment—"Mornington, Robert Cecil Mornington, lately attached to the *Rockingham* and now attached to you—I mean to your ship."

"Of course. And my name is——"

"I know it, Miss Susan Hubbell."

"I hope," she said, rising and turning toward the cabin, "that we may be very good friends, and again I thank you for your kindness."

She extended her hand to him, and this time,

before she divined what he was about to do, he raised it and pressed a longer and more fervent kiss upon it than the ordinary courtesies of life demand.

It was the first time that any human being had ever kissed Susan Hubbell's hand since she was a child, and for the third time in the course of an hour she found herself flying the English colors in her cheek as she received in astonishment this natural and ordinary salutation of a gentleman of her time.

CHAPTER XI

THE MAN OF THE WORLD AND THE CHILD OF NATURE

THERE is no place in which acquaintances are so easily formed and intimacies so rapidly developed as aboard ship, and the smaller the ship and the fewer the people, if there be the least congeniality between them, the more swift the growth of their knowledge and friendship. When the intimacy happens to be between persons of the opposite sex who are otherwise fancy free, it usually results in what this veracious chronicle purports to be—a love story.

For all her wide voyaging, totally inexperienced in the ways of the world and entirely unacquainted with masculine humanity in the guise of her captor, the association with the young man was novel and delightful to Susan Hubbell. He did not present himself before her with any advantage of position or circumstance. In the first place he came in the midst of a double grief caused by the loss of her father and the capture of her ship. The former she had as yet not fully realized. Captain Hiram seemed to her, not here to be sure, but just away. She had a fancy that if she should go up on deck, she would find him stumping along the weatherside and be met with his kindly smile and his hearty salutation.

Nor had she as yet taken in the full meaning that the *Hiram and Susan* was no longer her own. Everything went on just as it had been before. The ship's "doctor"—the cook, that is—happened to be a South American Spaniard and the cabin boy was his son. They had promptly volunteered to perform their duties and as they declared themselves Spanish subjects and their appearance bore out the declaration, they had been allowed to continue at their usual tasks by the Englishmen. Indeed, it was a great relief to Mornington, who was as fastidious about such matters as it was possible for a naval officer to be in those days—which after all was not much—that he was not compelled to subsist on the plain fare and the rude preparation of one of his own sailors upon whom perforce in the failure of these two to act, the lordship of the galley would have devolved. Save that she herself at Mornington's earnest request occupied the head of the table and he sat by her side, things went on at meal times, at least, much as they had before.

It was a good thing from one point of view that if she must be captured, Susan Hubbell had fallen into so kindly hands, for Mornington during the first week of her captivity exerted all his resources, which were great, to divert and entertain the forlorn but beautiful young woman of whom Providence had made him the guardian. He kept her, save when in the retirement of her own room, from dwelling upon her bereavement and her loss. And he did this in the most skilful way by making her talk about herself. The story of her life which he drew from her by degrees during the long hours of their pleasant converse as they walked the deck together in his watches was one that no other woman on earth could have told. Probably for strangeness and varied incident, it might indeed have been paralleled by the adventures of many a sailor, but in Susan Hubbell's case, these experiences were made doubly picturesque and attractive in that the subject of them was a woman.

Captain Hiram, so Mornington thought, must have been a rare character indeed to have brought up his daughter in such sweetness and simplicity and in such transparent purity in the

rude, womanless environment in which the life
of the two had been passed, and Mornington
felt himself aglow with gratification and thanks
to the brave sailor that he had had the courage
and wisdom to preserve this girl in the world yet
unspotted of it.

The unusualness of their conversation, the
unique character of the subjects discussed, the
unconventional frankness of the woman's point
of view, her innocent freedom of speech, which
yet never overstepped the bounds of true
modesty, lent to the acquaintance a remarkable
piquancy and the somewhat jaded taste of the
man of fashion and of feeling, if you will, responded quickly to the new stimulus.

Every woman who is loved is a new creature
to the man who loves her. There is novelty in
the growth of every passion else it would not
grow. To themselves no hearts ever beat as
these that throbbed within the breasts of each
pair of lovers in the great succession since Adam
looked on Eve and found her a new, a strange
and a delightful experience. But the acclaimed
novelty, however it might have been in Eden
was usually a matter of imagination, and
Heaven forbid that I should dispute the reality
of the imaginary. The baseless fabric of many
a vision is more firmly rooted than the house

built upon the rock. It is the concrete rather
than the abstract, the real rather than the ideal,
whose foundations are laid upon the sand.

But when there really was novelty, then a man
who met with it was like the quality of mercy
in that he was twice blessed. The sweet unaf-
fectedness and entire innocence of the world,
with the unusual mixture of vigorous and practical common sense and—I had almost said viril-
ity of character—as the mind of Susan Hubbell was unfolded before Mornington, were so
marked that sometimes he found himself wondering whether they were not after all the pro-
duct of that highest art which expresses itself in
simplicity. But it was impossible for him to
look into those beautiful eyes, without seeing
through those limpid windows into the honesty
of her soul. He found it impossible to look into
those same eyes without other consequences, too,
somewhat bewildering in their inward manifesta-
tions to the cool, experienced man of the world
that he flattered himself the association with
numbers of bright and beautiful women of his
own class had made him. Singular that the man
of the world should be made so by contact with
women rather than men, in his own fancy and in
the world's!

But a man of the world is never so much the

child of nature as when he is in love, and Mornington felt a bewildering consciousness that the impression which this woman was making upon him could soon be characterized honestly by no other description, if in some way he did not check the growth of those feelings which she engendered and stimulated in his soul. Having charge, dependent upon one's will and skill, of another human being, especially if that human being is a woman, is to stimulate by the subtlest of flattery, since it is usually unrecognized, that feeling of protection which brings people near together and develops the affections.

Any woman circumstanced as Susan Hubbell would have appealed to the man of heart and the man of honor alike. A gentleman would always have felt himself responsible for a woman in such a condition. And when to the ordinary instincts of a kind heart, a generous disposition and good breeding was added a sense of responsibility that came from the sudden deprivation of his charge's property and the imminent risk before her of a prison, the horrors and miseries of which to her he could well forecast, the situation called forth all that was best in the man. This was the more remarkable, too, in that the age was one in which women were regarded as fair game and men consciously or unconsciously assumed the position of beasts of prey with regard to them.

The more the lieutenant saw of his captive, the more determined he was that in some way she should be protected from the more rigorous consequences of the adverse fortune to which she had been lately subject.

She had never had any trouble in this world to speak of and she was only now getting her share. In the case of most of us, our allotted share of trouble is distributed through long periods and comes upon us, therefore, with less severe and overwhelming a mien. With Susan Hubbell, it had been thrust upon her all at once. There is a certain compensation in such a culmination, in that the human mind is not capable of realizing to the full such complete and sudden shocks. If the woman had been alone on the *Hiram and Susan* with no one but Mr. Conant and his clumsy attentions to break the edge of her grief, she could hardly have borne it, but here was a new interest struggling for dominance in her being, a new interest with all the advantage of novelty and youth on its side.

Ah yes, old affections must go by the board. The long love of years gives place to the swift attractions of an hour! The father and mother? these have been left while the young hearts clove together since Jacob served for Rachel, or since unhappy Cain took a wife out of the Land of Nod. Is the Land of Nod the country from which dreams may come, I wonder? So it was, although Captain Hiram had filled the horizon of his daughter's affections as full as any father could have done, there was a new seed implanted in the virgin soil, and another kind of love struggled beneath the sod, waiting but some sunlight touch to burst and blossom on the surface and take deep root down into the centers of being within.

The time was ripe for the woman to love supremely, the hour at hand that comes once in a lifetime. The time is always ripe for the man to love indifferently, but happily the supremacy of the one sometimes develops supremacy in the other affection, and then the couple are blessed of the immortal gods. When this does not occur, love is the prelude to sorrow for the woman. Susan met with so much warm and kindly sympathy, with such gracious and tender consideration, with such supreme and gentle tact, with such quick and ready response to the unconscious appeal of her situation, that she found herself basking in the attentions of the young man as a flower in the sun. Unversed in the meaning of those attentions, unaware that many of them

might be successfully simulated for evil pur-
poses, accustomed to take men, when she thought
of them at all, at their face value, the girl rejoiced in the intercourse with a constantly increasing delight which she took no great care to
mask or conceal—why, indeed should she?

Yet, she was not all a dreamer. There was
in her a substratum of hard and practical common sense, and because she was of quick and
fertile brain, there had come into her mind when
she noted the small size of the prize crew, the
possibility of the recapture of her ship. If that
recapture had meant the sudden breaking off of
the association between the lieutenant and herself, that possibility would have weighed heavily
in the determination of events. But a reversal
of conditions in which she were captor and he
captured was not without a certain charm. She
fancied fondly that it would enable her to repay
his courtesy and to meet his noble magnanimity,
and . . . But she hardly gave the subject
serious consideration, for unless there should be
concerted action between her and the crew lead
by Mr. Conant, upon whose fidelity she knew
she could absolutely rely, there would be no possibility of bringing about the desire.

And so while maintaining that hope in the
background of her mind, she allowed herself

to drift into an intimacy with the new captain of
her ship. At his earnest request, which he constantly repeated, she was prevailed upon to give
him much of her society. She spent long hours
on the deck with him during his watch; they
took their meals together in the cabin habitually.
There never was any one present, since the deck
could not be left without an officer and either
Merryfield or Mornington must always be in
charge. And the association, which seems
strange to tell of and would under other circumstances have been highly reprehensible, developed into a sweet and sudden intimacy, the
purport of which the man fully realized and of
which the woman would realize when the finish-
ing touch should be put by something that would
awaken her from her dream to the deep reali-
ties of her affection.

She had learned what little Mornington was
willing to tell her about himself. He was ex-
tremely anxious to know all about her and was
inexorably opposed to letting her know anything
about him, in which again in the microcosm of
the pair was seen the habit of the macrocosm of
the world. She did find out, however, that he
was alone in the world, with neither father nor
mother; that he lived when on shore at Alden,
which he described as a magnificent old country

seat, standing on the edge of the sea shore in Dorsetshire near Weymouth. From little indications that he had let drop, she surmised that he was poor, probably that he was a dependent upon the owner of the hall. She did not realize what a more experienced woman would have seen, that he had mingled on terms of intimacy with the *beau monde* of his day, for that was a phase of life upon which he dwelt lightly. But she was intelligent enough to delight in his manner and well educated enough to appreciate his mind, which indeed had been well trained, at Cambridge, before he entered the naval service. He had fought all through the American and French wars and could supplement her sea experiences with stories of high endeavor and heroic action, which like Desdemona she was glad to hear and for which indeed she loved him.

So while the ship sped on swiftly as the winds permitted toward the shores of England, these two drifted into positions from which presently it might be impossible for them to escape. The idyl is old and it took its natural course. The ship sailed true to its compass. The lovers drifted, giving no thought to final havens.

Into the Sea Paradise entered, not the serpent, but subtle suggestion from Mr. Owen Conant. Several times, regarding himself in honor bound

so to do, Mornington has sent for him and repeated his offer of quarters in the cabin subject
to the mate's parole. Each time the offer has
been disdainfully refused, greatly to the prize-
master's satisfaction.

On these occasions, Mr. Conant had enjoyed
the opportunity of exchanging a brief word with
Susan Hubbell, which in common courtesy
Mornington could not prevent, though he would
like to do so. From time to time also, Mr. Conant, when permitted with a few of the other
prisoners to take the air forward, had observed
the woman he loved and the man he hated pacing the quarterdeck side by side. The feelings of
Mr. Conant with such dual incitements may be
imagined. He was desperate, to put it mildly,
and was resolved to stop at nothing to recapture
the ship, to dominate the English officer and to
take that proper position he fancied to be his
own in the heart of Susan Hubbell. She herself was pointedly mindful of his situation. She
was not one to forget an old friend and she had
not hesitated to wave her hand or nod to him
when she found him looking at her from the
forward end of the ship.

CHAPTER XII

THE RUSE AND THE LETTER

ONE day, something like a week after the capture, it happened that Mornington was surveying the horizon through the glass, and the vigilant Mr. Merryfield had turned toward him in obedience to some remark, leaving Susan alone on the deck. Mr. Conant had been waiting for just such an opportunity, apparently, for, taking advantage of the free cover of the foremast, and while some of the original crew who were taking the air engaged the attention of the guards, he held up a piece of paper that to Susan's keen vision looked like a note.

Susan Hubbell felt very sorry for Mr. Conant, the more sorry because she found herself growing more and more interested in Mornington. She had hitherto viewed the mate's passion for her with indifference, but now a fellow-feeling made her wondrous kind, and revelling in, though but dimly comprehending, her own emotions, she felt a great pity for the sturdy young American sailor who could never be anything to her—and perhaps not to any one else—than the mate of a merchantman of which she was, or had been, the owner.

So that his obvious intent to communicate with her met with a readier response than it would have under other circumstances. At the same time, the little note made a powerful appeal to her curiosity.

Now, her affection for Mornington had not yet been precipitated. It was latent, inherent, trembling in the balance, as it were, but the spiritual reagent had not been infused into her being, and she did not yet grasp fully what it meant to her. She was aware of the pleasure she took in his society, and of the delightful emotions that filled her soul at the thought of him. She leaned toward him more and more consciously. In short, her love was like a bud which waits the kiss of the sun to burst into flower. And as it had not blossomed yet, it was sometimes more or less in abeyance.

The sight of that note checked the flood of her thoughts. The current of her being was turned backward from the man aft poised lightly near the rail, scanning the sea, and the idea of recapture flashed into her mind. It was possible—indeed, it was certain—that Mr. Conant would not risk communicating with her in this way for any slight purpose.

She rightly divined that should Mornington ascertain that a note had been delivered and received his displeasure would fall heavily upon the mate and he would be compelled, unless false to his duty, to abridge many of the privileges which had made the week so strange and so delightful to her. She was not disloyal to Mornington, for she had as yet professed no allegiance to him, partly, no doubt, due to the fact that the young man had not asked for any. For he, too, though with a fuller recognition of his feelings, was trembling in the balance.

In short, when Susan Hubbell saw that note in the hand of Owen Conant she determined to possess herself of it and then be guided by circumstances. Since she had been a captive she had remained abaft the mainmast. No restrictions had been placed upon her movements, but she had not thought it proper to go forward, nor had she desired to do so.

Although her captivity was made as little irksome as possible, she was still a captive, and she was not willing to subject herself to a possible recall or rebuke by venturing beyond the limits which instinctively appertained to her situation

and station. Her calm acceptance of her situation had thrown Mornington completely off his
guard. His infatuation—for he recognized it
as that if he should once let himself go—had
blinded him to any possibility of danger from
the woman he loved.

Delilah was the last person that Samson
feared, I doubt not, and here was no daughter
of the Philistines.

Susan turned and observed Mr. Merryfield
in somewhat animated discussion with his superior. A sail had been sighted to leeward, and
though it was more than likely to be a British or
a neutral ship, yet every sail in war time was a
potential enemy; hence Mornington's scrutiny
of the horizon.

The glass was passed back and forth between
the lieutenant and the midshipman, and finally
Mornington turned, and as it was Mr. Merryfield's watch and he was a great stickler for the
regular observance of routine, with a bow to
Susan and a brief word that he was going below for a better glass which he had observed in
the captain's cabin, he descended to the quarter-
deck and entered the cabin.

Mr. Merryfield had picked up the telescope
and was still staring down to leeward.

A rare combination of circumstances had created an opportunity for her. Susan did not hesitate a second. Making carefully certain that no one was looking at her, she unloosed the thin, flimsy bit of silk she wore tied underneath the collar of her loose sailor-blouse as a neckerchief, slipped far up to windward, and threw it high into the air. It was blowing fresh on the quarter. The wind caught the kerchief, and, guided by a prayer from her, carried it beyond the gangway into the waist. Had it not caught on one of the boom-boats, it might have gone farther forward.

The breeze was strong, and the cast of the silk, made with great skill, had been eminently successful. Quick as thought she ran down the ladder to the quarter-deck, making no sound as she went, and before any one could have stopped her—Mr. Merryfield being deeply engrossed and seeing nothing—she reached for the kerchief.

For one whose life had often depended upon the sureness of her grasp upon shroud or stay, she bungled unpardonably in the act of lifting the silk, and the wind whipped it out of her hand and blew it farther along the gangway, abreast the foremast. Instantly the mate picked it up and handed it to her as she came tripping after it.

"Avast, there!" growled the sailor on guard threateningly; "no gamming"—he was an old whaler, hence the homely sea phrase for conversation—" 'twixt the prisoners and this quarter-deck."

Mr. Conant looked at him as if he would like to kick him overboard, but he suppressed his wrath and remarked:

"I only picked up the lady's neckerchief."

"That'll do. Pipe down, now. Beg pardon, miss, but it's orders."

"Certainly; I understand," said Susan, turning and walking aft.

Nothing could describe the quickness with which, during the colloquy, she had disentangled the note from her kerchief and thrust it into her bosom as she tied the kerchief in place. When Mornington, who had got the glass and come on deck and noticed the group forward, arrived by her side—and he had run forward with astonishing promptness—she confronted him with an air of smiling innocence.

"What's all this?" the lieutenant began authoritatively.

"Your man was very rude to me," said Susan quickly. "I had unknotted my neckerchief, and the wind carried it out of my hand and blew it along the deck."

"From the poop to the fo'c's'l?" queried Mornington.

"It caught temporarily on the boom-boats," returned the woman quickly, "and just as I started to pick it up it blew free and Mr. Conant handed it to me, and then the man began——"

"What did you say to this lady?" thundered Mornington, his suspicions entirely diverted by Susan's cleverness.

"I—yer honor—I——" began the man, stammering.

"Answer me," persisted the lieutenant, now thoroughly aroused, but unfortunately aroused in the wrong direction.

"I didn't say nothin' to her, sir. I said no talkin' was allowed between the prisoners and the quarterdeck, 'ceptin' with you, sir."

"Mr. Conant didn't say one word to me," began Susan, with well-simulated indignation.

"I give you that parole you've been askin' for that I never said a word to her," put in the mate, blithely following the woman's lead and doubly delighted to deceive the officer he hated. "I jus' naturally picked up her kerchief, having seen you do the same sort of thing many times, and lookin' to you for information and example as to what a gentleman should do, as you once told me."

"Very well," said Mornington; "there has been no harm done, I suppose, only it looked a little out of order. No, I don't blame you," he said to the sailor; "you did perfectly right. Now, Mistress Hubbell, if you——" He indicated the stern of the ship with a gesture, and Susan quickly preceded him along the gangway.

Her step faltered and grew slower. She plainly waited for him, and though he was disturbed and annoyed and somewhat indignant over what exactly he could not formulate, he did not join her until she so pointedly halted that he, perforce, was compelled to do so. There was no one by the starboard gangway where they stopped, no one who could overhear, when she looked up at him and said, with real anxiety in her heart:

"You're not angry with me? I forgot I was a prisoner."

"No, child, not angry," he said reassuringly. "I confess I was startled, but you said he held no communication with you, and I understand it was all an accident."

Now, that was just what Susan had not said, and perhaps strict honesty would have compelled her to have explained that he had misconstrued her remark. And yet it was not her business to furnish him with constructions, she said to herself. If she told the truth, and he drew the wrong inference from it or put the wrong meaning upon it—why, that was his lookout. So she reasoned, and while she had a fleeting inclination to tell him, the moment passed and she was committed—and committed with an uneasy conscience indeed.

"You see, I never can be sure of a prisoner. The only one I'm certain of is the Frenchman in double irons. The mate has indeed given me fair warning that he will try to get back the ship, for, as you know, he has refused to give his parole a half-dozen times, and when I first saw you I thought you might be there by some contrivance.

Susan's lips trembled from a combination of motives hard to analyze and harder to define. She had been there because she wanted to be. She had contrived very cleverly to get there. She had in her possession, against her heart, a note which she felt morally certain contained tidings of moment.

She did not repent of what she had done, nor of the way in which she had done it, yet she felt a definite sense of personal dishonesty and of disloyalty toward Mornington. The very trust that he reposed in her, the readiness with which he had received her explanation and had allowed himself to be deceived, smote her keenly.

She felt like a traitor. She wanted three things at the same time. She wanted that note, and now that she had undergone so much and ventured so much to possess it, she wanted it more than ever. She wanted Mornington's respect, and she wanted to justify it. Lastly, she wanted her own self-respect.

Of the three desires, she was sure of nothing but the note. And with the choice plainly before her, she had chosen the note. Perhaps had she alone been concerned she could have fought down the temptation and have handed it to him then and there. Indeed, there came into her mind the fleeting intention so to do.

But she realized also that if the note contained anything incriminating—and the mere fact that so much had been risked by the mate to get it into her possession was evidence of its character—she would be betraying the mate and perhaps the men of the crew.

Like everybody else, once embarked on a course of dissimulation, every way spelled treachery and disaster. All this gave her a very troubled feeling indeed.

"I—I wish you wouldn't look at me that way," began Mornington as he saw the grief in her face. "No, no, I don't mean turn your face away from me altogether; that makes night where I stand. But don't grieve about it. It's all right. No harm's done."

"I know, but I am a prisoner—your prisoner."

"Sometimes, Mistress Susan, I want to forget that, and sometimes it's my sweetest thought."

He spoke softly, leaning over the rail and looking out through the open gangway in the ship's side. She could have won a proposal from him then and there had she been artful enough, or even had she been merely acquiescent, but she could not allow him to say a word of love to her while she had that note against which her heart was beating.

"I am your prisoner," she said, "no matter how you feel, and I shouldn't have left the quarter-deck, but I thought when the wind whipped my kerchief out of my hand that it was no harm to get it."

"There was no harm at all, my dear child," he returned promptly, with that air of paternalism with which he sometimes strove to disguise his anything but paternal feelings for her. "Say no more about it. I am ashamed to have brought any more trouble to you by what seemed my harsh words."

"They were not harsh. They were kind and generous, like everything else you have ever said to me. I can never repay you—never—never. I should have stayed on the quarterdeck or in the cabin."

"Don't say that," he began.

"I must. I will."

Her lip trembled. She was on the verge of a breakdown. Not because she was a woman given to tears on little occasions, but because the situation was fast becoming unbearable. The more magnanimously and generously he forgave her, and the kinder he became, the worse she felt. She was sure that she must terminate the interview immediately or else she would betray everything. So she resorted, for the first time in her life, to the old feminine form of evasion to escape. It was a case of instinct purely, not of training or habit—a reversion to type, perhaps.

"I—I don't believe I'm well," she faltered, who had never experienced a sick day in her life.

He was all solicitude at once.

"No," she returned, in answer to his protestations, "there is nothing you can do. I shall go to my cabin for a while."

"And you won't hesitate to call me if you

think of anything to help you? The ship is yours, you know."

He was not surprised at her profession of illness as he would have been had he been able fully to realize her abounding physical vigor and health, and so, on the plea that illness warranted it, he supported her along the deck and left her at the entrance to the cabin.

She went through the cabin and locked herself instantly in her own room, and then sat down on the transom, tore out the letter, and stared at it dry-eyed and shuddering. She had always had a high and splendid opinion of herself, but now she fairly reveled in her self-contempt and disgust.

If she had followed her first inclination she would have thrown the note out of the open port and thus have ended the matter, but that she did not do. It was the mate's secret, and she must know it. Whatever might be her course of action, she must read the note.

And so, with a beating heart and a furtive glance at the deck above, where her lover walked, as if perchance he might in some way observe her in the recesses of her cabin, she opened the soiled and tattered piece of paper which was the mate's only medium of correspondence.

CHAPTER XIII

AN OLD, OLD STRIFE

"At five minutes after four bells in the mid-watch, the midshipman's watch, we're going to take the ship. We depend upon you to look after the lieutenant. Lock him in his cabin or keep him below until we have attended to the men on deck and the *Hiram and Susan* will be yours in the morning. If you will help us, walk aft on the poop deck at six bells in the second dog watch."

That was the note. It was unsigned and written with a blunt carpenter's pencil on a piece of paper torn apparently from the fly leaf of a book. She now remembered that greatly to her surprise Mr. Conant had asked for a Bible a few days since. She had never known him to make use of the volume before, but she had said nothing when the request had been proffered, and this was evidently the purpose which he had in mind.

The note made an appeal to her which she

could not by any possibility disregard; and yet in the performance to which it committed her, she found herself unable to experience that joy and elation that should have been hers at the prospect of success.

She knew the mate, his courage and resourcefulness. What he attempted, he usually achieved. Her mind ran rapidly over the possibilities. The crew of the *Hiram and Susan,* including the officers, had numbered twenty-five. Captain Hiram did not believe in being shorthanded and he had never stinted his ship in service any more than in anything else. He found it paid in the long run to have enough hands to work the ship easily under all conditions. From that twenty-five, seven were to be deducted; three killed, the old cook and his boy, her father and the imprisoned boatswain François. That left eighteen Americans, so-called, under the hatches and available for duty if they could get out.

The prize crew from the *Rockingham* which had been bound East on a long cruise and did not desire to deplete her own complement any more than she wanted the incumbrance of prisoners in the hold, numbered twelve men and the two officers. Six of the men would be off watch and asleep in the forepeak, one officer would be below in the the cabin; Mr. Merryfield in whose watch the uprising was to be made would of course be aft on the poop or quarterdeck, one man would be at the wheel, one man would be forward on lookout in the forecastle, two would be on guard at the hatch leading to the space below decks beneath the forepeak in which the prisoners were quartered. This would leave two men in the waist. These two would probably be dozing. The rest would be awake and alert and heavily armed. The men in the forepeak were available almost upon instant call. Against the watch would be eighteen men of the crew led by the mate, whom she knew to be a hardy, enterprising man who did not know the meaning of fear and who was as strong as a bull. There were no arms among them. They would have to depend upon naked fists or such chance weapons as they could come at in the shape of pieces of plank or broken stanchions, if there were any to be had. There was not even a sheath knife left among them.

The weather conditions were favorable. There was no moon and there was every promise of a freshening wind. It was a good top-gallant breeze as it was and should it come on to blow harder, as was likely, the ship would probably be under single-reefed topsails. That was an advantage for it eliminated from the game the man at the wheel. Unless the wind direction changed, the *Hiram and Susan* probably would be on the port tack. In that position she knew from experience that her ship steered heavily and required constant watching. To let go the wheel would probably rip a mast out of her. She reasoned, and the mate she divined had reasoned the same way, that the man at the wheel being a sailor before anything else would instinctively cling to the spokes and hold the ship steady whatever happened. Thus the men on deck available for defense against the attack would be reduced to five and the boy. The boy was brave and resolute, but only a boy just passed sixteen years of age. Still he was a factor to be reckoned with. He would be a rallying point for the others.

She did not know what the details of the mate's plans were, of course, but she realized that practically the success or failure of the whole enterprise depended upon her, for if a man of the lieutenant's courage, daring and skill and with his vivid and impressive personality entered the fray, he could probably rally his men, if they were taken by surprise, and frustrate the attempt at recapture. Or if he did not succeed in that, there would be a bloody and frightful conflict on the decks in which—her heart con-

tracted suddenly—Mornington might be killed.
She estimated him correctly and knew that if
there were any fighting going on, he would be in
the very thick of it.

Singularly enough, that swift consciousness
which projected the lieutenant there, was one of
the greatest arguments, had any been needed, to
commit her to the plan in its entirety. With the
sophistry of affection, she persuaded herself that
she would be doing him a possible good turn in
the saving of his life by preventing him from
coming on deck. The possible danger to him—
and in her imagination she saw him stretched
lifeless on the deck, and singularly enough it was
always by a blow from some weapon in the
hands of Mr. Conant that this was accomplished—was the illuminating touch necessary to reveal to her the actual condition of her
heart. The dreadful picture had been the reagent
which precipitated an instant mental avowal
that she loved him more than she had ever
loved anything before and in a way so different,
with a feeling so strange and unusual that she
was utterly at loss to describe it. Her experience afforded her no basis for comparison. The
wild surge of her heart as the realization burst
upon her was like to nothing less in her mind
than a tidal wave.

She dropped the note, clasped her hands to her breast and turned pale from the very violence of her emotion. Whatever happened, whatever occurred, she would love this man through life, through death, beyond! A great passion speaks various languages, but the gift of tongues is always conferred upon one who has been blest with a conception of it. To love greatly is to live grandly and perhaps to die nobly. The sphere of life and the form of death are of little moment. The one may be passed in a hovel and the other may be experienced on a cross, what matters it? In the eye of truth these things are of no importance as love is there. Wherever she might go, whatever she might do, whatever she might be, this girl suddenly and in truth becoming a woman to the very full, knew that she would be possessed with an eternal and undying passion for this man.

The thought might have brought shame to a more complex and artificial nature—and complexity is generally artificial. The natural is simple and simplicity is the aim of Nature since it began to act upon the world of God. If she had been a different woman there would have been humiliation in the avowal even to herself of this great passion, when there had been no corresponding avowal at least openly to her on the part of the object thereof.

At first she was only concerned with her own emotions. There was enough that was new and startling in them to occupy her to the full. Presently she would realize that a passion which is not met and matched is after all like a bird who flies awry because of one lamed or broken wing. But then her mind had not room for two consciousnesses and that she loved him was enough. Loving him now in this way without reserve and realizing it without delusion, could she assist in the recapture of the ship?

There was first of all the question of property. The ship did indeed belong to her and by every law of God or man she was justified in retaking her own, yet that statement did not weigh with her a single moment. She would have given up a thousand ships for the welfare and happiness of the man she loved.

She realized that the capture of the ship would be first a blow to his pride; that it would be a serious blot upon his professional fame; that he would be held strictly accountable for the loss of that which had been committed to him. Could a woman who loved a man as she loved Mornington fail to allow such considerations to weigh heavily in the determination of her action? If they were all that could be urged, she would throw the note overboard, find some means to tell the mate that the scheme had been discovered and that he must abandon it and let things go on as they were, warning the man that she loved of the necessity for increased vigilance.

But that was not all. Susan Hubbell was an intensely patriotic woman. The manifest did not show it and the mate did not know it. It was a secret her father had shared only with her. In addition to the cargo of general merchandise, silks, wines, jewelry, bric-a-brac, etc., the *Hiram and Susan* had stowed away a number of cases of small arms, muskets, pistols, swords, and among these several boxes which contained a subsidy of a million francs in gold from France to the Congress and to General Washington in America, to say nothing of a number of important papers and public documents of great value.

Nor did the silks and other cargo belong to her or to her father. They were consigned to certain merchants in Boston. The arms were for the Continental Army whose long struggle for liberty was about to be crowned with success and the money was for the pay of the troops. She had no moral right to dispose of these things.

Above all things, Susan Hubbell was a right-
eous woman to whom duty was habitually the
foremost consideration. That stern New England conscience had been an heritage which she
had enjoyed to the full limit. As an honorable
woman, as a patriot and as a lover of her country, she would have been stamped with shame ineffable had she failed to do everything in her
power to secure the delivery of the cargo, the
arms and the subsidy, to those to whom they
were consigned. And as it has been since time
and the world began, Love and Duty tugged at
the heart strings, and Honor cast his weight into
the balance and Love fell back conquered.

There were minor considerations, of course,
trust reposed in her good faith by the mate and
the men, the thought that she had no right by
her actions to condemn them to the horrors of
the British prison ships. These all had weight
with her, but the determining factor was that
powerful sense of duty to her friends and above
all to her country. Although it caused her agony
of spirit, she could no more have decided against
her conscience and in favor of her heart than she
could have killed Mornington with her own
hand.

She had made up her mind with the singular
boldness of her rearing and environment that she

would teach Mornington to love her. She would not have been a woman at all had she not realized that he was greatly interested in her, and she was confident that so great a wealth of affection as hers would presently evoke an adequate response. It would have been easy, so ran the thoughts of her untutored mind, if things had gone as they had for her to accomplish this. She knew nothing whatever about social conventions, and that Mornington might be influenced by them and might shrink from allying himself to a sea-waif such as she was even if he loved her had never entered her head.

But now the situation would be materially and tremendously changed. Her action would put him in that position which she instinctively felt no man could possibly endure without resentment. The resentment would be toward her and possibly from one point of view, he would have some right to be angry with her, but whether he had right or not, he would still be angry, bitterly so. Whether she could make him see the position as she saw it, she did not know. Naturally, she hoped so. Indeed the revelation of her affection had been so deep and sudden and overwhelming that in her heart she could never conceive the possibility of an ultimate failure to do anything with him that she liked.

And really she was not bound to him. He had exacted no parole from her. He had given her the run of the ship and allowed her to do just what she pleased. It was his business to have taken precautions and to have put her upon parole or to have locked her up, or . . . But these considerations, correct though they were, did not drive away the uneasy feeling of treachery.

However, whatsoever her thoughts and desires were, her course was clear. She must assist the mate and the men as she had been asked. Having come to this decision, being the intensely practical woman that she was, she began to think how best she could carry out their plans.

CHAPTER XIV

THE UNANSWERED QUESTION

ALL that the mate asked from her was that she should in some way detain Mornington in the cabin. How could that be done? It was by no means an easy problem. She did not know whether he locked the door of his stateroom when he turned in or not, although it was probable that he did not. Under the circumstances it was more than likely that the door would simply be on the latch; for, she reasoned, if he were summoned, or if it were found necessary to send for him, the minute or two of time that would be required to get him awake and have him unlock the door might mean a lost ship. Therefore, she decided that the door would not be locked. There was only one way to secure it from the outside. She would have to get the key and lock it herself. It would be easy to take the key now when no one was in the cabin and secrete it, but if she did so it was barely possible that he would

notice its absence and inquire. Once his suspicions were aroused, the attempt at recapture
would be useless.

To open the door and take the key while he
was asleep would be a risk, but there was nothing else she could think of. Nothing is gained
without risk and this was the point of hazard
in her endeavor. Having locked him in, what
would be her next move? Being committed to
the enterprise, she might as well do as much as
in her lay to make it a success. She thought
deeply and at last came to a conclusion.

There was the natural relief in her mind at-
tendant upon a settled question, and as it was
now late in the afternoon, she prepared for action. First she read the mate's letter over carefully several times to be sure that she had made
no mistake as to the time and signal. Yes, it
was clear. At six bells in the second dog watch,
she was to turn from the break of the poop
where she would be standing and walk directly
aft to the taffrail. Some one of the crew would
be on deck and would report to the mate, if he
were not there himself, that she had comprehended and would do her part. Then she tore
the paper into little bits and thrust out her hand
through the open port and scattered them in the
sea.

Being now embarked on her course, she resolved to carry it out with boldness and spirit, and as she heard the door of the outer cabin open and the familiar footfall of the lieutenant, she opened the door of her stateroom and came out into the cuddy.

In a few moments it would be supper time. Four bells had just struck ending the first dog watch and Mr. Merryfield had just relieved his superior, who did not go on duty again until eight. Mornington's first question as he entered the cuddy was for her health. The sight of him had brought a wave of color into her cheek, and the sight of her completely reassured him. He took her hand in his own and kissed it. How he loved to kiss that firm, strong, shapely, if somewhat sunburned, hand. She had got used to this performance by now; not that custom had dulled the pleasure she took in it. On the contrary with her new consciousness, it had never seemed so sweet to her as at that moment. He still held it as he raised his head and she did not make the slightest effort to withdraw it. You see she had not learned the art of coquetry and she knew no better.

"You are quite well?" he began, solicitously.

"Perfectly," she answered smiling brilliantly and endeavoring to speak indifferently, although her heart went nigh to choking her. "I'm so ashamed of myself. I don't know what it was . . ."

"So long as it's gone, we won't waste time upon it," said the young man smiling infectiously. "You don't know how anxious I have been about you during the whole of my watch. If anything should happen to you . . . why, it would be worse than losing the ship."

"Do you mean a great deal by that?" asked the girl.

"Do I?"

"I mean, does it . . . would the loss of the ship be very much to you?"

"There is only one thing on earth the loss of which would hurt me more."

"And what is that?"

He took her other hand and drew her slightly toward him. She did not realize what he intended, or if she did, she was not quick enough, or perhaps she had no desire, to prevent his action, for he bent his head and kissed her full upon the lips. How she met that kiss she did not know. The blood rushed to her face and then ebbed instantly. She stared at him, pale, her eyes bright like stars. He would have done it again, had she received it after the ordinary method to which he was accustomed, but there was something in her gaze that stopped him.

"Forgive me," he faltered at last feeling desperately uneasy at what he had done, although she had neither stormed, nor raged, nor wept, nor smiled.

He released her hands as he spoke and as if he had been her support in this crisis, she sank down upon the transom and buried her face in her own hands while the wild beating of her heart which had almost stopped when he kissed her, sent the blood surging into her cheeks again. And all the while she said no word, for all the while within her soul, fierce, wild turmoil was raging.

"He kissed me and he loves me!" she murmured to herself. "He kissed me on the lips and he is mine and I am his. The horror of the loss of his ship is measured by his love for me, and I can understand what that is by mine for him. And I must take it away from him . . . that ship. He did not weigh it in the balance with me, but when the crisis comes, what then? He kissed me and I am his. I belong to him. Shall the slave rebel against the master?"

She took her hands from her face and clutched at her breast staring at him again where he stood shamefaced, contrite, and yet inwardly exulting at the divine touch of lip to lip which had been his a moment since.

"What does it mean?" faltered the girl.

"It means"—he hesitated and threw prudence to the wind—"it means that I love you. Have you not divined it? Has it not been eloquently spoken to you with every voice since the day I saw you, since the moment I laid my hand upon your shoulder, when you wept here in the cabin, and without knowing why or what, I felt so strangely attracted to you . . . a lad! It means that I have forgotten everything; that you are . . . an alien, of another country, the enemy of mine; that I have been . . . your captor. It means now that the positions have been reversed and that I am yours with all that I am, and all that I have and all that I shall be. I love you! I could say it over and over again and not say it enough."

"It means that you love me?" she asked, breathlessly, as if she could not take in the tremendous significance of those simple words. "It means," she repeated softly to herself, lingering over the delightful phrase, holding up a warning hand as he stepped nearer to her, "that you love me. It cannot be possible."

"Would that you could look within my heart

and see how rare, how fervent, how overwhelming is my adoration for you!"

"And you are mine and I . . . "

She stopped again and before her rose the determination of the hour.

"Say on," he urged tenderly, coming closer, and as was the fashion of an older day when proposals were not made at the theater, or in the automobile, or on the golf links, he sank down beside her on one knee and took her hand within his own. "It means all that to me, that I love you," he said. "What does it mean to you?"

"And you are mine, my very own. You want to marry me and have me for yourself all your life?"

"For all my life!"

"An alien, a stranger, an enemy?"

"It makes no difference what you are, or whence you come, or how you describe yourself. It's you . . . you . . . that I love."

"And you are mine?"

"Yes, and you?"

She drew herself away and rose to her feet, breaking the abruptness of her movement by reaching out to him a helping hand. If she had consulted her inclination, she would have thrown herself into his arms and have clung to him as if they could never be parted. Her lips would have sought his own, her heart would have beat out its story against his breast, but now the inexorable decision, the unalterable course that she had determined upon rose between them.

"I did not anticipate . . . I did not expect that you would care . . . so soon," she began.

"Then you have thought of it?" he questioned swiftly seizing the intimation. "You do love me?"

"Don't ask me now," she answered desperately, determined to end the interview at all hazards since she felt that she could scarcely support it longer. "Don't ask me now."

"But I must have an answer. A man doesn't lay his soul in a woman's hand to leave it there unknowing."

"You shall have your answer to-morrow. Have pity on me. I am your prisoner and I really can stand nothing more now."

"To-morrow then be it," returned Mornington who saw that the girl was almost at the breaking point, and who had tact and kindness enough not to press the matter further. He would have been a fool if he had not seen that she loved him. Though he begrudged with the parsimony of a lover toward his mistress

even a day without an answer, he was strong
enough to give her that time for which she
pleaded.

Habitually he wore his sword at his belt in
which his pistols were thrust. On duty and in
this warlike guise, he had made his avowal and
declared his affection. To him too had come
the completing touch in the hours of the only
watch that he had spent on the ship in which
she had not in some measure shared, save when
the mid-night period fell to him. Without her,
thinking of what would happen to him if that
illness should prove serious and she should be
called away—and although he was in no condition to marry anybody unless that somebody
were rich and of station to match his own, and
although every voice except that of affection
bade him stay while there was yet time—he had
thrown all such restraints to the winds and allowed the passionate devotion of his heart free
rein in guiding him whithersoever it would.

He looked at Susan, lovelier than ever in her
agitation, and bowed his head.

"You are overwrought," he said tenderly, "I
should not have spoken so soon or so abruptly."

She put up her hand to stay him. He could
never have spoken too soon or too abruptly
about his love for her. But he went on:

"I shall leave you now and to-morrow we will talk over this again."

He took her hand once more and kissed it as he had never before kissed the hand of a woman. She thrilled to the passionate imprint of his lips upon her hand. He straightened up, unbuckled his sword belt, laid it with his pistols upon the table, bowed to her as ceremoniously as if he had been at the Court of St. James's and entered his own cabin.

Action is the surest alleviation of desperate thought. Although her body was shaking with the feelings that had been brought out by that passionate half hour, she realized that here was an opportunity that would stand her in good service. She lifted the belt quickly and drew the pistols from their holsters. At first she only thought to take out the priming, but he would probably look to that before he went on watch again. She would have time, she thought, if she worked rapidly, to draw the charges. She stood close to his cabin door and could hear him splashing in his wash basin preparatory for supper—so closely allied are the petty conventions and habits with the greatest crises of life! Again she was taking a fearful risk, but again the end justified the means and her endeavor was achieved. She knew all about weapons, which would have been unfamiliar tools to most feminine hands, and she drew the charges, shook out the powder and ball, thrust the pistols back into the holsters and fled to her own stateroom before he came out.

She refused to join him at supper that night, but took her tea and what else she forced herself to eat at his earnest solicitation, in her own room. Just before six bells, she went on deck whither he fain would have followed her, save that she motioned him away. She felt that she could not trust herself even to speak to him now. As she climbed to the poop, she saw the mate forward, apparently idly staring aft. She knew that he was noting her every movement keenly. She stopped at the break of the poop and after exchanging a word with Mr. Merryfield, she looked forward listlessly.

Mornington had introduced man-of-war customs on the *Hiram and Susan* and at seven o'clock the bell forward was struck sharply six times in three couplets by one of the seamen. She hesitated a moment for the action of the next minute absolutely committed her to the endeavor. She might even at this last hour refuse it. If she made no movement, the mate would know that she declined to do her part and he would naturally suspect that under the circumstances the attempt would better be abandoned. It seemed to her that she waited for hours, but it was only a second after the clanging of the bell reached her ear that she slowly turned and by as iron an act of self-compulsion as ever was put upon a woman, dragged herself slowly aft, where she stood looking over the taffrail.

It was done in a moment. A few steps and she felt as if the course of her life had been irrevocably changed, as if she had committed herself to a course of action which might wreck her eternal happiness. "One false step often does that for a human being," she thought bitterly as she turned and went below, again passing the lieutenant who sat quietly in the cabin thinking of her, when perhaps he should have been thinking of his ship.

CHAPTER XV

TRIUMPH AND DEFEAT

THERE was a chronometer in her cabin which Susan kept carefully regulated by that belonging to the ship. As the hands approached the hour of two o'clock in the morning, she rose and made her final preparations. For the first time since she had met Mornington, she was dressed in man's attire. She had blushed and shivered with shame as she put it on and her changed emotions well typified the great transition through which she had passed, but she rightly judged that skirts would hamper her in what she proposed to do.

The mate's note had allowed her five minutes. That would be ample, she thought, and she resolved not to begin until the bell struck four. She stood, therefore, at the door of her stateroom, holding it slightly ajar, waiting until the two couplets came faintly to her ear in the night. Then she slowly opened the door and entered the cabin.

There was a light burning dimly in the cabin, but it was so placed against the forward bulkhead as not to throw any rays into the stateroom she was about to enter. A step brought her to the door of the stateroom occupied by Mornington. She had in her hand a stout piece of whale line with which she intended to try to lash the door in case she should find it locked. During the first watch, while the lieutenant was on deck and Mr. Merryfield was asleep in his room, she had taken the precaution to oil the hinges and locks so that the opening of the door would give no warning. Like most sailors, she knew that Mornington was a light sleeper and would easily be awakened by anything unusual in sound or touch.

She placed her ear against the door and listened. She thought she could make out the sound of his deep and regular breathing, but she was by no means certain as to that. She turned the handle of the door softly and with an exquisite delicacy of touch and then she opened the door a few inches and listened again. This time she was sure she could hear his breathing. To her great relief, he was sleeping soundly. She reached her hand around the side of the door and there was the key in the lock. To withdraw it was the work of an instant. So far she had been brilliantly successful. Nothing remained now but to close the door and turn the key. A man would have done that without hesitation, but for all her clothes, she was not a man. With the key in her hand, she opened the door farther and peered in. It was doubly foolish because she could see nothing except the dim outlines of a figure in the berth and if the sleeper had chanced to wake up, everything would have been discovered. His good angel must have been sleeping also, for he did not awaken.

Full of disappointment that she had not seen him more clearly, she carefully closed the door, inserted the key, and turned it in the lock. There was a distinctly audible click as the bolt shot to. She waited a moment again, with her heart in her mouth to learn if he had heard the sound, although now that the door had been locked, it would be impossible for him to break it down in time to be of much service. Of course, if his pistols had been in order, he could have blown the lock to pieces, but she had reasoned that it would take a few minutes for him to discover what was happening, a few moments more to find the door, some time to get his pistols and discover they were unloaded and still more time to light his lantern and charge them again. By the time that was done, the attempt would have succeeded or failed, and he might do what he would in either event so far as she was concerned. He did not wake up, however; his continued breathing assured her of that.

Laying the key down on the transom, she opened the outer door and stepped out on the quarterdeck. A half gale of wind was blowing, a fine rain was falling and it was as black as pitch. She had not made a sound in opening the door and the man at the wheel, peering into the dimly lighted binnacle to watch the wavering, swinging compass and holding the ship steady on her course in spite of her mad jumping, did not see her. His attention was so fixed upon his duties that he had neither eyes nor ears for anything else.

She had slipped off her shoes in the cabin and crept softly up the ladder. She had left the cabin by the lee door, as she had surmised the midshipman in charge would be well up to windward. He, too, was peering forward into the smother of the rain and mist and darkness with every sense on the alert to see ahead. She gained the poop deck without making a sound. She dropped to her knees as she did so and sheltered by the rail crawled aft until she was well back of Mr. Merryfield. Her heart, which had beat so furiously in the presence of Mornington, was steady now. She was as cool and quiet as she had ever been in her life. She rose to her feet and with catlike tread stepped across the deck and judging that the five minutes had now elapsed, she flung herself upon the midshipman, caught him by the shoulders and with all the strength of her powerful and vigorous young body, hurled him back upon the deck. He came down with a resounding crash. His head struck a ring-bolt and he rolled sideways and to leeward and lay still.

The noise of his fall awakened Mornington in the room immediately below. She thought she heard him moving, but Susan recked little of that. Taking no care in the excitement of the moment to ascertain how badly the midshipman might be hurt, and believing that he had only been badly stunned by his hard fall—which proved, indeed, the case—she drew his pistol from his belt, whipped his sword out of its scabbard and sprang to the ladder.

At the same moment there came to her a shriek and a cry from forward, followed by the sound of a pistol shot, mingled with the splintering of timber. The man at the wheel raised his head and stared forward as if petrified. Susan could now hear Mornington making a tremendous uproar back in the cabin, beating and pounding upon the bulkhead and losing valuable time in shouting. The men at the gangway had started to their feet at the noise and had also run toward the forecastle. She followed quickly after them. There was a confused huddling mass around the fore-hatch. Sword out, she ran the nearest of the English seamen in the back with the point. The wound was not dangerous, not even severe, but it had all the moral effect of an attack in the rear.

"They've got the ship," roared the man, dashing aside and yelling with pain. "I've been stabbed in the back."

The diversion was all that was required to enable the mate and two or three of the most energetic of the American crew to make good their stand on the deck. The mate had succeeded in breaking into the hold. The men below had got at one of the arm chests and by some means they had contrived a battering ram out of a stanchion. The first blow had shattered the hatch, and although the man on guard had shot the first man who sprang up, the mate, who was abreast of him, had run the sailor through with a bayonet. Two or three had gained the deck and the mêlée had begun when Susan arrived at the end of it.

It was all done so quickly that the men off watch in the forecastle also awakened by the tumult and the shouting, had scarcely gained the door when they found it shut against them. They made a great commotion, but harsh voices bade them be still if they valued their lives, as the ship was now in the possession of the Americans. The whole eighteen had poured out on the deck and the four surviving British sailors of the watch—one of the six being desperately wounded and perhaps dead, and the man at the wheel completing the tally—had been securely lashed to whatever place came handiest.

"Well done, Miss Hubbell," cried the mate exultingly, as he realized the success of their endeavor. "What become of the leftenant?"

"I locked him in his cabin."

"Let's go aft then. Four of you guard the fo'c's'l there," cried the mate. "You've got the Britishers' pistols and cutlasses. If any man sticks his head out the door, blow it off of him. Now, Miss Susan. Come along the rest of you."

Followed by a huddle of men, the mate and the girl ran rapidly toward the quarterdeck.

"Two of you look after that man," said the mate pointing to the helpless man at the wheel who dared not let go and was forced to submit tamely to capture—and indeed resistance then

would have been folly—"Give me his pistol.
That's well. The rest of you stand by for a
call. Come, Miss."

The two entered the cabin. As they did so,
they were met by a dull, muffled roar. The
door of the lieutenant's quarters flew open violently and Mornington half-dressed, stepped
through the smoke into the room. He had at
last re-charged his pistols, blown off the lock and
entered upon the scene of action—too late! The
first thing that caught his eye through the smoke
was the mate. In an instant the lieutenant had
him covered with his remaining pistol; holding
it as firm as a rock in his left hand, he reached
back where he had rested it leaning against the
bulkhead, and caught his naked sword.

"Ah, Mr. Conant, have you come to the cabin
to give me your parole?" he began with his
usual urbanity.

"I've come to the cabin to take charge of the
ship," said the mate.

"Well, you'll not take charge of it just yet,"
returned Mornington confidently. "For if you
lift your hand or move from where you are, or
even raise your voice, I shall be under the painful necessity of putting a bullet through your
brain."

The mate laughed, taking care, however, not

to move. As would have been said in another age, Mornington "had got the drop on him," and for all his levity, the Englishman was not a man with whom it was safe to trifle for a moment. So the mate stood strictly at attention without making any effort to close with the officer. He could talk, however, that at least was not prohibited, and although he was no match in the conversational game for the lieutenant, he felt this time that he held winning cards, and he would be very stupid indeed not to be able to play the hand to advantage.

"You might as well put up your pistol," he began.

"Allow me to be the judge of that."

"Oh, of course, I'll simply lay the facts before you, and then you can decide whether you want to act like a fool, or . . ."

"Like a gentleman?" interrupted the lieutenant, who was enjoying the situation.

"Just so," said the mate calmly enough, although inwardly growing more and more indignant every minute. "The ship's mine. We've killed one of the watch and captured the other five, shut up the rest of the crew in the forepeak and you're all that's left."

"And Mr. Merryfield?"

"He was lyin' on the deck nice and quiet

when I heard from him last," sneered Mr. Conant, laughing.

"You dog!" cried the lieutenant, stepping
forward as he did so, "I've a mind to pistol you
on the spot."

The mate shrank back. There was not a
drop of cowardly blood in the American's
veins, but Mornington's face was so con-
vulsed with rage and he was so furiously angry that the mate's life hung in the balance of
a hair.

"I can end you any way," continued the lieutenant.

"And what'll my men do to you, if you do?"
said the mate. "The ship's mine and . . ."

"No," said a voice, "it's mine."

"You! Good God!" cried Mornington, turning to the corner of the cabin whence the voice
of Susan Hubbell had come to him. She had
shrunk back against the bulkhead behind her
companion, when she saw the attention of her
lover was fixed upon the mate, and in the dim,
smoky room, he had not noticed her before.

That one glance in her direction was fatal to
him, for Mr. Conant seeing his opportunity,
sprang upon him the instant his eyes were avert-
ed, with the quickness of a tiger. The pistol
was wrenched out of his hand before he real-

ized that he was attacked and the mate swept his arms about him and held him so that he could not use the sword. Physically the lieutenant was no match for the gigantic New Englander. He struggled desperately a few moments, but unavailingly. The mate's hand reached down and got the sword. He tore it from the lieutenant's grasp and threw it across the deck. In a moment more he forced the officer down upon a transom and stood over him threateningly.

"My compliments," said Mornington, when he could get his breath, "on your strength, Mr. Conant. Faith, I was as helpless as a child in your grasp."

The mate laughed grimly.

"Bigger and better men than you have tried it out with me and with much the same result," he said.

"I suppose so. Now, what are you going to do with me?"

"Curiosity," said the mate severely, "ain't quite the thing for a gentleman, I take it."

"Now, Mr. Mate," said the lieutenant, suavely, "it's bad enough to be captured without having to take lessons in manners from such as you."

"You gave 'em to me, or tried to."

"You needed them. I don't," returned the officer coolly.

"Will you let Mr. Mornington alone," cried Susan Hubbell, furiously.

"Oh, very well," surlily assented the American. "Meanwhile we'll lock him up in one of the other cabins unless he's willin' to give his parole."

"No more than you were," said Mornington indifferently. "Which cabin have you selected?"

"That one," said the mate, pointing to an unused stateroom on the other side. "In with you."

"There is some compensation in a prison," said Mornington, gracefully rising to his feet and stepping toward the cabin, "in that it relieves me of the necessity of looking at you"— he paused, staring straight into the blackness of the little, empty stateroom—"and other persons on this ship," he added with cutting deliberation and unusual emphasis.

It was his sole and only allusion to Susan Hubbell. After that first exclamation, he had not noticed her in the remotest way.

Mr. Conant shut the door, locked it, picked up the piece of line that Susan had left on the floor and lashed the handle of that door to that of the door next to it, "to make assurance double sure." Then he turned to the girl.

"Miss Susan," he said, "you done the job up handsomely. But for you, we'd never managed to pull the wool over that leftenant's eyes, and I congratulate you upon gettin' back the ship."

"I hate you!" cried Susan. "I loathe you, I despise you, I want you to get out of my cabin at once and not speak to me again until I give you permission!"

She turned on him like a wounded lioness. Such was the fury, fire and passion in her voice that the mate shrank back appalled.

"But . . . Miss Susan," he began.

"Not another word, not another sound! If I had a weapon, I believe I would kill you here!"

The mate backed toward the door open-mouthed, trying to speak and utterly at loss for words before such a tornado of feminine fury.

"Didn't I tell you not to say anything to me?" she cried, approaching him menacingly. She felt almost as if she could have sprung at his throat and grasped it in her hands.

The moral courage of the mate was not proof against such an attack. He turned and left the cabin precipitately.

Susan stood in the room, staring at the door, with heaving bosom and panting breath. Then

she turned and walked back toward the door of
the lashing. She hesitated, then she put her
hand on the knob.

"Mr. Mornington," she cried softly, and
then loudly. Next she shook the door; then she
beat upon it with her hands and called his name
again and again, receiving no more reply than
as if she had been hammering upon the entrance
to a tomb. Finally she sank down upon the
deck and fell against the door in complete abandonment and burst into a flood of sobs and
tears. But the man in the stateroom, who heard
it all, paid no more attention than if the sound
that told of the breaking heart upon the other
side had only been the creaking of the ship.

CHAPTER XVI

HE LOVES ME, LOVES ME NOT

ALTHOUGH he had put a brave face upon it in the cabin before his captors, the sudden reversal of conditions and the entire change in the relationship between himself, the ship and the woman, fairly appalled Mornington. He stood erect in the dark room into which he had been thrust a prey almost to despair. So engrossed was he in his own gloomy reflections that he did not hear the first outburst from the woman he loved, and it was not until she had spoken several times that he realized that she was denouncing the mate. He did not at all comprehend the meaning of this outbreak of bitter wrath. His first thought was that the mate had offered her some familiarity or indignity and he turned fiercely toward the cabin with an instinct to help the girl. A second thought checked him, however, even if the locked door had not intervened. She was abundantly able to take care of herself, he realized, and whatever was happening, she had brought it upon herself. Besides he presently heard the discomfited mate stumble out of the cabin.

He listened acutely for what might next occur and was of course aware of the first touch of her hand upon the door of his prison. He heard her call him by name and her piteous appeal to him to answer. Next he realized from the shock against the door that finally she had fallen against it, and once more he started toward it with the intent of bursting it open, thinking that possibly she had fainted, until the sound of her long drawn sobbing assured him that she was still conscious, and then his bad angel took him in hand.

Against the terribly affecting appeal thus made to him, he steeled his heart. He had never loved her so passionately as at that moment perhaps, when he considered that they were irrevocably parted by a treachery and ingratitude which broke his own heart. He had taken her for absolute sincerity, for artless innocence, for childlike transparency, and behold, not the most finished coquette whom he had ever met in all his life had so thoroughly and entirely deceived him. She had, in fact, wrapped him around her finger. She had flirted with him outrageously;

played with him, led him on to a declaration of love and by a base, ignoble pretense of reciprocating his feeling had fooled him to the top of his bent. He burned with the humiliation of the thought.

The mate had recaptured the ship by what means he could not tell, and in the recapture, Mornington's professional honor was seriously jeopardized; his hopes of preferment in his profession utterly blasted. He would have to face a court-martial when he got home, if he ever did get home, and the result would be his ruin. It showed the intensity of his feeling and the depth of his newly awakened love for Susan Hubbell that he scarcely gave this phase of his situation a thought.

His mind reverted again and again to the woman and not to the ship. He had enjoyed large experience among men and women. Though young in years, he was already a man of the world, a shrewd, careful observer of events, a reader of character. Last night he would have staked his salvation on the honesty of this girl, and now to what pass she had brought him by her trickery and chicane. Indeed, he had staked his salvation from a professional point of view upon her. With what result was now painfully apparent. He swore, listening all the while to that low, choking sobbing outside the door, that he would never speak to her or look at her again; that he would tear her out of his heart and drive her from his thoughts.

He reproached himself bitterly for allowing himself to be cozened, cajoled, deceived by an inexperienced girl. He raged savagely against the artificial conception which he had fatuously entertained concerning her. He assured himself that he was glad that she wept at his door; that he rejoiced in the evident abasement which kept her there; that he hoped and prayed she might realize her shame and dishonor, a greater dishonor, manlike he thought, than his own.

Not six hours ago, in that very cabin, he had kissed her upon the lips and she had not withdrawn herself from that caress. He could have sworn that the kiss was returned. She had promised him he should have his answer on the morrow, and behold, he had got it that night. He had been in a fool's paradise of his own creation, and had awakened to find himself on blasted, sterile earth outside of Eden.

Unthinking, scarcely realizing, he broke into a sudden, harsh and bitter laugh. The woman outside heard that laugh with all its mockery and self-contempt and scorn. It smote her like

a blow in the face. It came to her bitterly that
this was the only answer he had vouchsafed to
all the plea she made crouching against the door
and weeping her heart out. It stopped her sobbing instantly. Her face flamed with shame
and wounded pride. Outraged womanhood as-
serted itself, temporarily at least. She rose to
her feet, dragged herself to her own cabin, flung
herself down on the berth and lay there dry-
eyed, choking, panting in agony. She had lost
him, lost him forever just when she had loved
him and he had loved her. The cup of joy that
had been held before her lips had been dashed
down; not even the dregs remained to be drain-
ed. That cold, cruel, merciless laugh nearly
killed her. Sleep she had none, tears more she
had none. She lay there wrestling with despair
the long night through.

And he was in scarcely better case himself.
The low moan of pain outside his door which
had woven in and out his thoughts stopped as
suddenly as a clock stops when a hand is laid
upon its pendulum; stopped, he realized, coincident with, or consequent upon, his laughter.
The sudden cessation of the sound of what had
almost been a death cry startled him. The current of his thoughts ceased. He listened. He
heard her rise slowly, her footsteps fade away,

while the faint echo of the sound of a closing
door came to him. She had gone, and then—
silence and darkness harder to face than the low
cry of a moment since.

He had mocked at her grief in his heart,
whelmed her with contempt in his soul, yet the
fact that she had been there he now realized
had been strangely comforting to him. She had
deceived him, betrayed him, ruined him, yet she
was perhaps sorry. It flashed into his mind that
the mate had offered her no indignity and that
she was raging against the position inexorable
in which she found herself, and womanlike had
vented her anger upon the unwitting cause of it.
He had even a grotesque touch of sympathy for
the mate, lost in an instant when the sudden
thought came to him that perhaps what Mr.
Conant had said about his future and that of
Susan Hubbell had some basis in fact.

Instantly, upon the idea, he decided, with a
passion of jealous rage at the conclusion, that
the woman loved the mate. Therefore, it was
the more evident that she had been playing with
him, Mornington. He locked his teeth together
and clenched his hands. If the mate had come
into the door then, I fear me his great strength
would have stood him in little stead.

For no matter what his resolution, no matter

what his determination, no matter how he might despise what he believed to be her treachery, Mornington knew that he still loved the woman and the knowledge filled him with shame. He knew that if he carried out his intention never to speak to her or be with her again, it would cost him his life, and there was added humiliation to his pride in the thought. Believing in her treachery, he argued that loathing and contempt for her should be his proper feeling. But lo, although he could not, and would not, and did not forgive her, he loved her just the same. He thought if she had asked him for the ship, that she might have had it for a kiss. Indeed he would have given the ship, everything but his professional honor, for his old faith, and his old trust, and his old belief in the woman that he must love forever, unworthy though she seemed to him.

His passion for her burnt like a sun. She was the focal point of his solar system, and when the sun itself had grown cold and dead, if life eternal were given to him, he would still be aglow with love for this woman—this woman, whom, God forgive him, he ought to hate! Oh, that she would come back to the door and call his name again! He would tell her that it did not matter, if she could only prove to him that

she had not played with him when she had trembled upon the verge of an avowal responsive to
his own in that very cabin a few hours before;
if she would only tell him, explain to him, whatsoever the mainspring of her action might be,
that she did really love him, he would take her
to his heart again and adore her in return.

But no, she had deliberately ruined him. She
had sought and gained his love only to betray
him. If he had kept her a rigorous prisoner
and allowed her no privileges unless safeguard-
ed by parole—a woman's parole, a woman in
love with someone else, he thought bitterly, tearing at the shirt he wore as if it constricted his
heart—if he had taken these precautions and
she had outwitted him, it would have been a
cause for mortification and humiliation perhaps,
but it would not have broken his heart. But he
had given her every liberty, every freedom; he
had never restrained her or questioned her in
the slightest degree, and he had given her his
heart of hearts, his very soul. The giving meant
much to him. It meant nothing to her.

And yet—and yet—and yet! her picture rose
before him; her eyes looked upon him; her
hands clung to him, the fragrance of her lips
was in the air he breathed. He could have
sworn that she had loved him—and yet she had

betrayed him! He loved her; he hated her; he despised her; he worshipped her. And he too flung himself down on the berth and wrestled through the long watch with all the demons of pride, and suspicion, and anger, and jealousy, and hate; like the woman separated from him by a few thin bulkheads waiting and hoping for the dawn.

Joy is said to come with the morning. Would it ever come to those two storm-beaten hearts on the wave-washed, wind-tossed, water-borne ship?

CHAPTER XVII

THE SWEETS OF THE VICTORY

The *diabolus ex machina*—as both the lovers would have phrased it, if they had spoken Latin —the mate, who had perforce kept the deck the rest of the night, came below into the cabin at six o'clock, determined to have some sort of a settlement of the questions which had annoyed and perplexed him. He committed the deck to the Greek, in default of any better seaman, for the short time he expected to remain in the cabin.

The Spanish cook and the Spanish cabin boy had accepted without the slightest evidence of feeling this latest change in the mastership of the vessel. Their business was to cook and it was a matter of indifference to them under what flag they prepared their savory messes for the cabin and their unsavory messes for the crew. So that the mate found breakfast laid as usual in the cuddy.

It was a cold, raw and rainy morning. The
wind had increased, the storm clouds were low-
ering blacker than the night before and the ship
was pitching heavily close hauled in a half gale.
Mr. Conant, of course, could not take an observation. He had had no opportunity to scan
the log-book. He had not the slightest idea
where the ship was, but he knew that his way
lay toward the west, and the *Hiram and Susan*
had been headed as nearly in that direction as
the wind permitted ever since he had taken the
deck. If the sun came out, he would find her
exact position and lay out a course which would
bring them to Boston Harbor, whither they had
been originally bound. For the present, all they
could do was being done.

The cabin boy was bringing a smoking coffee
pot from the galley when Mr. Conant knocked
on Susan Hubbell's door. She had heard the
boy bustling about and the clatter of the dishes
as he laid the table. She had also heard the
gruff word of greeting addressed to him by the
mate at his entrance, and knew what to expect.
There was no reason why she should not meet
the mate; in fact, she had to meet him, and the
sooner it was over, the better. She rose, therefore, in answer to his knock and bade him wait
a moment, that she would be out presently. She

did not take the trouble to change her attire. Why should she? What difference did it make what she wore or how she looked now? She did freshen her face and hands with water, however, and then she entered the cabin.

"Good morning, Mistress," began Mr. Conant.

"Good morning."

"You wasn't feelin' right well, I guess, last night?"

"No," answered Susan, quietly, "I was not—and perhaps I owe you an apology for my wild words, but I was overwrought, and—"

"Don't apologize, Miss Susan," interrupted the mate, who was not without his finer feelings, "jes' say that you didn't mean that you hated me and I'll forget all the rest."

"Certainly," said Susan wearily, "I don't hate you. Why should I? I—I'm grateful to you," she faltered, "for restoring me my ship."

"Well," said the mate, "you done the most of it, the most important part of it yourself, in takin' care of the leftenant. If he'd been on deck or got on deck soon enough, 'twould have been another matter."

He spoke loudly, as he always did, without the slightest intention of being overheard, without the slightest thought of it, in fact. But

Mornington, listening keenly, heard every word and raged the more at this plain confirmation of his suspicions.

"Don't say any more about it," said Susan swiftly, "I'm mortified, ashamed."

"What, to get back your ship?"

"No, no, you don't understand. What shall we do now?"

"I've laid our course as near west as the wind'll let us, and soon as I can get hold of the log and get a sight of the sun I'll fetch away for Boston. That I take it 'll be your wish."

"It will be the only thing to do, I suppose," answered Susan evasively.

"And I thought p'r'aps you'd come up on deck with me after breakfast and we'd work out our sights together if it clears, which it don't look like it, and mebbe you could arrange to relieve me for a watch so's I could get a little sleep. There's no one to take charge of the deck, 'cept the Greek, that is, and I don't dare trust him out of my sight a half hour."

"What are you going to do about François?" asked Susan, with a shudder of horror at the thought of the murder of her father.

"I've got him in irons for'ard, and under guard, such as it is. I can swing him up to the

yard arm now, or carry him into Boston and turn
him over to the law."

The mate's face gloomed as he answered. His
enforced sojourn in the forecastle in close association with the cut-throat crew had enlightened
him more with regard to the character of the
men before the mast on the *Hiram and Susan*
than all the rest of his experience. He felt absolutely alone amid a crowd of blackguards, with
a woman to protect. The swift and sudden
changes of command and the death of the captain had disorganized the crew to a high degree.
They were restive and impatient, ready to break
out. He must keep them down with a heavy
hand, and he was heavily handicapped in his
endeavor by the presence of Susan Hubbell.
Alone he could have faced anything undaunted.
She complicated the situation terribly. And the
imprisoned murderer made matters worse. Mr.
Conant would have hanged him out of hand had
he not feared that the slightest attempt at such
summary action on his part would have precipitated an outbreak among the men with whom
François was very popular.

"I suppose it is proper to take him to Boston," said the girl slowly and with reluctance.

"Yes," answered the mate, "and now what's
to be done"—he pointed to the door of the

stateroom in which Mornington was confined—
"with him?"

"Why, I should say the first thing is to let
him dress himself, and give him some breakfast,
and then—"

"One thing at a time, Miss."

Mr. Conant stepped over to the door, cast off
the lashing, pulled the key out of his pocket—
and it flashed into the mind of the girl that re-
taining the key as he did showed that he had evidently a lack of faith or trust in her, but she said
nothing as he turned the lock and opened the
door.

"You can come out now, Mr. Englishman."

"So long as you are out, I think I prefer to
remain in," returned Mornington, with his usual
aggravating nonchalance.

"Prisoners are allowed no preferences on this
ship," returned the mate grimly. "You'll obey
orders or take the consequences."

"And what are the consequences, if I do
not?"

"Me," answered the big American tersely.

"I've felt your prowess before, Mr. Conant,"
remarked the lieutenant, lightly, "and I believe
this is a case where 'discretion is the better part
of valor.' Since I needs must, let me at least
do it gracefully."

He rose from the bunk and stepped toward the door of the cabin. He was one of those men whose good looks are independent of his clothes, and although he wore neither coat nor waistcoat and his shirt was torn to rags as the result of his struggle with the mate last night, he looked as handsome and as distinguished and bore himself as jauntily as when he had first set foot on the deck of the *Hiram and Susan.* A greater contrast to Mr. Conant could scarcely be imagined, and yet they were both men in whom an unprejudiced observer could take pride and satisfaction. The American, tall, strong, deep-chested, massive, rugged, stern; the Englishman, graceful, agile, alert, distinguished, courageous and possessing a certain high and proud bearing which made the sturdy New Englander seem plain, even humble, before him.

Although Susan stood just back of the mate and Mornington's eyes comprehended her equally with Mr. Conant, there was not the slightest recognition of her in them. Yet his heart had leaped in his bosom at the sight of her, as hers had risen at the sight of him. She had half started toward him, the color rushing into her face, when she met his steely, indifferent, unknowing glance and shrank back, turning pale and biting her lips as she did so.

"Now that you have me here, what next, Mr. Conant?"

"Clothes," said the mate briefly. "Into your cabin yonder. You're in no state to stand before a lady."

"A lady?" queried Mornington sweetly.

The mate growled like an angry bear and stepped toward him.

"A lady," I said. "Yonder!" He swung his hand back toward Susan.

Mr. Mornington raised his eyes from the deck below to the deck above in the blandest indifference, comprehending Susan from head to foot in one contemptuous stare. Seeing, he would not see. And the woman writhed inwardly under his frankly manifested contempt of her.

"I see no dress, no ribbon, or furbelow," he continued blandly.

"Damn you!" roared Conant, raising his fist. "Do furbelows and dresses makes ladies with you? Well, I'll learn you that—"

"Stop!" said Susan, interfering. "Unless you wish my everlasting enmity, don't lay the weight of your hand on that man."

The mate drew back; Mornington, as before, taking absolutely no notice of the girl, and indeed bearing himself almost as if the whole affair were a matter of extreme indifference to him.

"Clothes is what you need and then breakfast. Yonder's your cabin. Dress yourself and be quick about it," Mr. Conant choked out, his hands clenching and unclenching in nervous menace as he stood near the lieutenant.

To get to the door of his cabin Mornington had to pass very close to Susan Hubbell. She was humiliated beyond measure at his scornful indifference. Her pride raged in her breast. She thought to show him a like contempt, but as he approached her with his head in the air, carrying off all the honors, although at such a terrible disadvantage, in the interview, her heart drove her toward him. She stepped almost in front of him and half extended her hand. He did not see it. Indeed, he did not notice her any more than if she had been incorporeal air.

The mate, who had not observed this little byplay in his rage, tore at the neckcloth he wore as if it were choking him.

"That man fills me with such hate that I can hardly keep my hand off of him," he gasped out hoarsely as Mornington disappeared.

"And I tell you again," repeated Susan emphatically, "he is to be let alone."

"Will he give his parole?"

"I don't know."

"What's to be done with him?"

"I don't know that either, but we shall see when he comes out. I—I wish you would hurry the breakfast," she began. "Won't you call Manuel?" she went on to gain time to break the dreadful situation.

The mate stepped to the door, went out on the quarterdeck and presently came back, followed by the cabin boy on the run. When the mate called in that mood there was no lingering in obedience.

The breakfast, smoking hot from the galley, was set upon the table. Places were laid for three. The mate rapped roughly on Mornington's door and roared out, "Breakfast."

The lieutenant had been surprisingly quick about his toilette, for he immediately came out of the cabin, fully dressed, smiling and serene.

"Your place," said the mate, pointing. "Yours, Miss Susan. And this'll be mine."

He stepped toward the head of the table.

"That's my place," said Susan sharply. "I own and command this ship. Sit there."

The mate had about all that he could stand. His eyes rolled fiercely, his teeth locked together, but again he submitted. He would not permit the Englishman to enjoy an open quarrel, and he saw that Mornington's eyes were taking in every detail of the situation, while his lip curled significantly.

Now it had been the practice of Captain Hiram and Susan to say grace before meals, and the practice had been kept up throughout the week of her captivity by Mornington, who had complied with her first request that he do so half in jest, and who had continued it because he liked it. As the three ill-assorted people sat down, Susan hesitated.

"Mr. Conant, will you say grace?"

"Not me."

Her glance sought the lieutenant. She did not dare to address a word to him, but he was equal to the occasion.

"The duty, I perceive, of asking a blessing upon mine enemies devolves upon me, but at least there is Scriptural warrant for it. For what I have received and for what I am about to receive, may the Lord make me truly thankful," he went on with bowed head, and the girl was fully conscious of the sarcastic touch in as strange a petition as ever prefaced a meal.

The breakfast was partaken of in absolute silence by all. After that irreverent prayer, Susan could not bring herself to say a word and the mate had no inclination to conversation. Pride kept the lieutenant equally silent. Susan could eat nothing. Everything she attempted to swallow choked her. The mate, after the plain fare of the forecastle, made great play with the dainties of the cabin. Mornington, who wanted food no more than the woman he loved, resolutely applied himself to his breakfast to show her his indifference, and she hated him the more for that. Under such circumstances, the meal was soon over.

They waited while Manuel cleared the table and until he withdrew.

"Now, sir," began the mate, laying his heavy fist upon the table with no very gentle emphasis, "what about you?"

"Is there anything about me that needs discussion, sir?"

"Everything. But I mean what are we going to do with you? Curse you!"

"Gently," interposed Susan quickly.

"As I conceive it, Mr. Conant," said Mornington, still ignoring the woman, "that is a question the settlement of which you have reserved to yourself. I appear before you as a spectator, a listener, a learner, interested if you will, but having nothing to say in determining the matter."

"Will you give me your parole not to attempt to recapture the ship?"

"Never. If I can take her again I shall certainly do so."

There was a snap in the lieutenant's eyes and a set to his jaw when he said this that indicated the intensity of his desire and his determination.

"Forward you'll go then with the jacks in the fo'c's'l."

"No," said Susan Hubbell; "he stays here."

"But, Miss Susan," blurted out Conant, "he made me go forward when I wouldn't give my parole."

"That's different," said Susan recklessly.

The mate's face flushed.

"Why different?"

"I don't care to explain. I've told you a dozen times that I own this ship and that I intend to command her. Now, you can carry out my orders, or—or. There is no alternative," she went on, rather lamely. "Lieutenant Mornington stays here."

"Locked in his cabin, then," said the mate.

"That's as may be. At any rate, you will give me the key."

If it had been a man who had spoken thus to Mr. Conant he would have received a very different answer, but there was something in Susan —or was it in the mate?—that compelled his obedience. He had loved her ever since he had

known her, and that had been for all the years
he had sailed with Captain Hiram, but he had
never felt that he had a chance of winning her
until the death of the old sailor had somehow
thrown her into his hands. He was shrewd
enough to know that she would never give her
hand where her heart did not go, and he realized
that if he balked her or crossed her, with her im-
perious temper and in her present exacerbated
mood, she would hate him. It was best for him
to humor her. Without a word he handed over
the key.

"It's dangerous," he remonstrated. "If he's
at large without a parole he'll take back the ship,
or he'll make the duty of watchin' him a terrible
task with the rotten crew we've got, to say nothing of the murderous dog for'ard."

Rotten crew! Mr. Mornington started a little at this. Rotten crew! If he could only get
among them with his own sturdy tars.

The mate had seen the involuntary movement
and regretted his indiscretion.

"Have it your own way," he said to Susan,
"only I warn you. You fooled him once"—the
girl actually shuddered at this blunt declaration
—"don't let him fool you in turn. He can have
the run of this cabin. I'll see that an armed
man watches the door, and let him put a foot

outside at his peril. You command the ship, but
I'll transmit your orders to the men, and some
day you'll find out—who is—master." The
words came from him against his will.

"I'll have you know that I am master now,"
said Susan. "Now go! I will see you presently."

Her own anguish made her cruel indeed. The
poor mate had deserved better treatment at her
hands. He had given her her liberty and her
ship, although she herself had largely contrib-
uted to both results, and she should have had
kind words for him instead of censure and blame.

Mornington had watched the episode with
curious interest. His first feeling was of relief.
There surely was no lcve lost between those two.
At least, it was evident that Susan cared nothing
for the man, although the mate's desperate passion was to be read of all men. In the next moment dark suspicion clouded his mind, for he
wondered if this were a comedy got up for his
benefit. Whatever he thought, he sat perfectly
silent. She would have given the world if he
had commenced the conversation, but he waited,
as a prisoner should, for her to begin.

"Mr. Mornington," she commenced falteringly, "I—I suppose you can't understand—"

He bowed gravely.

"You don't know—some explanation is due you."

"Madam, I ask none."

"You—you—you asked me a question last night."

"I have received my answer. Let me see, it was at four bells in the mid-watch that the reply came to me in unmistakable terms."

"Then you think that I—I—"

"I don't permit myself to think about you at all," he returned indifferently. "If you are curious to know my thoughts, they are about the loss of the ship and the means whereby I was—betrayed."

She shrank back under the cutting cruelty of his words, simple enough, but filled with an implication she could hardly sustain. She did not know what to say or what to do.

"You—you have the freedom of this cabin, if you wish it," she began, "and I shall arrange that you may go on deck on occasion."

"Under the circumstances," he answered, rising to his feet and towering over her tall and stately while she fairly cowered by his side, "I prefer to be quite alone. I find my own society," he went on with a bit of pardonable—shall I say—boastfulness, "better adapted to the needs of a gentleman than that of boors and"—

he paused to give the word due meaning—"co-quettes."

He turned on his heel without another word or glance, entered his cabin and shut the door, leaving her sitting where she was, stretching her hands out to his departing figure in vain, in hopeless and heartbroken appeal.

CHAPTER XVIII

SUSAN HUBBELL remained below in her cabin, a prey to her own melancholy reflections, till dinner, which indeed she partook of alone. By afternoon it was impossible for her to remain in seclusion any longer. She would go mad, she felt, if she were not doing something. Presently then she dragged herself to her feet, wandered aimlessly out of the cabin to the quarterdeck. She was startled as she passed through the door to see a seaman on guard. The ship looked much as it had before, save that the familiar figures of her own crew replaced the British sailors. They had been sent forward under hatches and in the places occupied but yesterday by the Americans. The fore hatch had been recovered and there was no evidence of the mêlée. The two wounded British sailors were being cared for by their shipmates. Mr. Merryfield, whose hurt had proven not serious, had been peremptorily sent below with the men by the mate. Susan had not given him another thought in the excitement of the interviews in the cabin, and there had been no one to insist that he be allowed quarters aft.

The mate was pacing the poop nervously as Susan came on deck. He caught sight of her at once, stopped and looked entreatingly at her, although he did not venture to address her. In obedience to the obvious invitation in his glance, she turned and climbed the ladder to his side. He motioned her back out of the observation of the man at the wheel, and, of course, as they were alone in the poop, no one could hear what was being said.

"Miss Susan," he began desperately, for he was desperate, "there's somethin' I've got to say to you, somethin' you've got to hear."

As usual she resented the imperative mood in him, as she did in anyone unless it might be in Mornington, who refused to talk to her in any mood at all. But the mate's earnestness and a certain curiosity to hear what he had to say, the tenor of which she had begun to suspect, restrained her from voicing her objection.

"You know me, Miss Susan," began the mate awkwardly. He was more master of himself when handling the ship than when pleading his cause with a woman, it was evident. "I sailed with you an' your father for a long time now. I ain't got much education, but, if I do say it myself, I'm a prime seaman, a good navigator and an honest man. I'm an American, too, an' heart and soul agin England and the Britishers. Now, you're here alone in this world, your nat'ral protector bein' gone, and I'm the captain of the ship. I takes charge of the ship, save, of course, your rights. Why shouldn't I take charge of the girl with the same proviso? I'm young yet; I can make myself anything you'd like to have me, if you'd only help me and gim'me a chance."

"Mr. Conant," began Susan calmly, although this manly avowal had not failed to awaken at least a new respect for the mate in her heart, "I know your good qualities thoroughly. I realize that it is to you that I am indebted for my present liberty and the restoration of my ship"—alas, that thought brought to her mind other things for which she most unjustly felt that she was indebted to the mate, womanlike forgetting for the moment her own share in them—"and I'm deeply grateful," she went on, forcing herself to the word, "but I don't love you. Until lately I've scarcely known the meaning of the word," she continued wearily.

"Until lately?" said the mate eagerly. "Since when, may I ask?"

"You have no right to question me," returned Susan, "and I know of no reason why I should answer, yet I will. Since the capture of this ship by the *Rockingham*."

She was a strange girl and recked little of conventions, else she would never have made the avowal.

"You don't mean to say that you love that English pop-in-jay?" said the mate hotly, his dark face reddening.

"If you refer to him in my presence again," said Susan decidedly, "remember that he is a gentleman and try to be one yourself."

"That for his gentility," snapped the mate. " 'Cause I ain't got his fine manners and his soft words and his black heart, damn him! I can't win you."

"If you continue in this strain I shall refuse to hear another word."

"Wait!" exclaimed Mr. Conant, stretching out his hands to bar the way. "I don't know what I'm sayin'. You needn't think 'cause a man don't wear fine clothes and speak fine words that he hasn't got a heart in him. I love you with every drop of blood in my body. I'd die for you. Would he do more'n that?"

"I don't know," faltered the girl.

"I never dreamed of this," continued the New Englander. "I thought you was jus' foolin' him, leadin' him on with the intention by and by to seize the ship."

"He thinks so, too," said the girl, "and he refuses to speak to me or to have anything to do with me."

"An' you love him? Great God! it can't be. The enemy of your country, the captor of your ship, a man who insults you by refusin' to speak to you, who mocks and disdains you!"

"Stop," cried Susan. "Do you love me any the less because I don't love you? Do you care any the less for me because if you say another word in this line I shall hate you? What difference does it make to one who loves what happens, or how that love is received? Is your love the kind that depends upon anything but what's in the heart to grow? Do you think it doesn't mortify me and humiliate me and break my heart to love a man who mocks me, who cares nothing for me, who, without permitting me a word of explanation, believes me guilty of the basest treachery and ingratitude? Oh, that my father were here! He would understand."

Susan could remember no mother. She had never felt the sympathy that lies in a human

mother's heart for her child. Her mind reverted only to that stern old father.

The mate was utterly abased by this display
of feeling. He recognized truth in what she
said, in that, although she admitted frankly that
she did not love him, her mere elusiveness and
unwillingness, the impossibility which she plainly
declared of returning his affections and the frankness with which she discussed the real bent of
their direction, only made him love her the more.
He groaned in spirit as he looked at her, the
beautiful and the unattainable woman.

"You're right," he said hoarsely. "Love
goes where it's sent. After all's said and done,
the ship must go with the wind. I can't help it;
you can't help it. I'm sorry for you. If I
didn't love you as I do, I should be sorry for you
'cause you ain't loved by the man you've given
your heart to, and if I didn't even know you and
had jus' heard about you, I'd still be sorry for
you, 'cause you're an American and the man
that's first in your heart is an enemy to your
country."

"Pity is all I can expect, perhaps it's all I'm
worth," said Susan sadly.

"You're worth the best of everything that
goes," said the mate earnestly, "an' while I'm
very far from bein' the best mate on the seas

perhaps, I'm goin' to try to be somethin' that perhaps will make you think more of me and less of him."

"It will be useless."

"I don't know about that.   There's nothin' to prevent my hopin' anyway."

"Hope!" said the girl, throwing out her hands, "it's dead in me.   No more!" she interrupted as the mate opened his mouth to say further, "I came up to take the deck and relieve you.   You've had no sleep since night before last, and if the ship is to be brought safely to harbor you can't be spared."

"I can go another day and night, I guess," said the mate gratefully, touched as he was by her solicitude.

"No, I'll keep the deck until nightfall and do you go below and get some sleep."

"The leftenant?" queried the mate.

"Locked in his cabin."

"And the key?"

"Here," said the girl, laying her hand upon her breast.   Would, she thought, that she possessed the key to the prisoner's heart instead of that to his place of ward!

The mate sighed deeply, unbuckled the belt around his waist and tightened it until it was more of a size for Susan, to whom he handed it. From it depended a sword and two pistols, which the mate himself had carefully charged.

"It looks as if it might come on to blow harder," he said, "an' if it gets more threatenin' I'd take some of the canvas off her and get another reef in the tops'ls."

The ship had her fore and main-top-gallant sails set over a single reef in the topsails.

"Ay, ay," said Susan, "trust me for that."

"An' another thing," continued Mr. Conant, "I don't trust that gang of blackguards and cutthroats we've got on board farther than I can see 'em. This change of flags an' capture and recapture an' so on, an' the death of the captain, has unsettled 'em mightily. They're ripe to rise and take the ship for themselves. I've no doubt some of the gang may have tried mutiny or even piracy before. And we know François is a murderer. So keep your weather eye liftin' an' at the first sign of trouble rap on the deck for me. I'll hear you and come a-runnin'."

"Have they any arms?" asked Susan.

"Only the men guardin' the cabin and the two watchin' the fore-hatch."

"And who are they?"

"The most reliable of the ship's company, but not much more to be trusted than the rest."

'I shall keep a sharp lookout," returned Susan confidently. "Now, go below and turn in."

"Thankee, mistress," said the mate, "an' don't you have no hard feelin's agin me for speakin' out. I can't help loving you, an—"

"It's all right," said Susan impatiently but not unkindly, "and you're wasting time talking to me when you might be asleep."

There was no help for it. The mate had to get some sleep and there was no one else to leave in charge of the deck, at least, no one whom he could trust with the ship and with the crew. The French boatswain might have done well enough on the score of ability, if he had not stabbed the captain, but he was certainly the most depraved villain of the lot, and the Greek was scarcely any better.

Susan had stood her watch about an hour before the Levantine came aft with three or four of the men. She stepped to the break of the poop to meet them, motioned them not to approach the latter from the quarterdeck.

"We want to speak with you, Miss," began the Greek in his broken English.

"Stay where you are," said Susan, quietly laying one hand on the pistol at her hip, although she did not draw it, "and say what you have to say."

"We want to know who's responsible for this ship and where she's goin'," said the sailor roughly.

It was an unheard of breach of sea etiquette for him to have taken that action. As he spoke she noticed that the men about the decks, save for the two guarding the hatch, had left their stations and were now coming aft to hear what was going on and to lend the moral support of their presence to the impudent interrogation.

To the sturdy, stubborn courage of her New England ancestors, Susan Hubbell added the bold daring of the ancient Viking race from which she sprang. She saw that the seamen had no arms except their sheath knives. They were within easy range of her pistols and they knew, for she had often practiced at a mark before them, that she was a sure shot. She could account for two of them without moving from the poop before the mob could take a dozen steps, and with her small sword she could keep the rest of them at bay, if they did not at once give way, until the mate could gain the deck. She was entirely cool, therefore, and not in the least degree agitated; in fact, in the fierce distress of her soul, she rather welcomed a chance for action. She had never killed anyone, of course, and save for the men who had fallen in the capture of the ship by the frigate, she had never seen anyone killed, else her view of the possibilities of the situation would have been vastly different.

"You have no right to any information whatsoever," she said coolly, "and I decline to give you any."

"We didn't ship to be commanded by no woman," growled out one man, an Italian, whom they had picked up at Bordeaux. "We shipped for a cruise to Boston under Captain Hubbell."

"Ay, ay," cried another.

"And he's dead," continued the Greek.

"Yes," said Susan sternly, "murdered by one of you."

" 'Twas a shot from the frigate," exclaimed one.

"Release François," demanded a third.

"We took back the ship ourselves," cried a fourth.

"An' we're goin' to know where she's goin' an' all about her, an' we ain't goin' to serve under no woman," broke out another voice.

"Where's Mr. Conant?" cried still another seaman. "The cabin boy told us that you said he'd got nothin' to do with the ship, and we'd like to know how you come to be in command?"

Quick as a flash Susan whipped out the pistol. She covered the men with it instantly.

"I own this ship," she said quietly, although her voice did tremble a little. It was well that the trembling was restricted to the voice and not the hand, which held the pistol as steady as a rock. "When my father was murdered by François she became mine. And the bo's'n shall hang for his crime, too. The mate is my mate. You are my men. I shall do what I please with my own."

It was not apparent whether she referred to the mate, or to the crew, or to the ship, but her meaning was evident enough.

The Levantine swore loudly; a deep growl came from the rest of the men.

"This," said Susan, decisively, "is mutiny. You will go forward to your stations at once or I will put a bullet in you, Georgios, and at this range one shot ought to account for two or three of the cowards behind you. You've seen me shoot at a mark, and you know that I don't miss it."

"But," began the Greek, his eyes rolling horribly.

"Not another word. If you are not off the quarterdeck and dispersed instantly I shall open fire, and if this mutiny is repeated I shall release the English officers and the English sailors, and we'll see who will have the ship then."

The Levantine, mad at being thus braved by a woman, lifted his fist and shook it at her. His life, too, hung in the balance of a hair.

"You fool," cried another sailor, dragging him back, "don't you see she means business? You'll be shot like a dog. Forward all of you." He turned and led the way. The men moved slowly at first and finally broke into a nervous run.

Susan laughed contemptuously at the frightened rabble and thrust the pistol back into her belt. Raising her voice, she called out loudly:

"I've something more to say. The first man that steps abaft the mainmast without orders will be shot dead. Now, don't forget that."

One woman had for the time being cowed a whole ship's company. It was a triumph surely, but in that triumph there was a terrible foretaste of eventual defeat. She would not always be in such a position of vantage, and the men whom she had so mercilessly humiliated and scorned would at last have the ship.

Not once did Susan relax her vigilance throughout the long hours of the afternoon. The sky gave ominous portent of the coming storm, but still she held on, held on with every bit of canvas that had been set, until the men, and there were good seamen among them, wondered uneasily when the order would be given to reduce sail. They knew that if a storm broke upon them with everything all standing the *Hiram and Susan* would be stripped and dismasted, if she were not forced over on her beam-ends to founder in an instant. Susan was not unmindful of the weather. She wanted to teach the men a lesson and she, therefore, took the long risk necessary to impress it upon them.

Presently toward five bells in the second dog-watch, the Levantine and one other sailor, the Italian, came aft. They stopped at the main-mast before the woman's warning upraised hand.

"Beg pardon, ma'am," began the Italian, whose milder nature better fitted him to act as spokesman, "but there's a deal of wind off yonder, and if it breaks on the ship with the canvas on her—"

"I told you that I was in charge of the ship. Get forward."

"But, Miss—"

"Get forward!" she cried more sternly than ever.

There was no resisting that voice and air and the firm hand on the pistol. The two men turned and went dejectedly forward; hatred such as few men have ever felt for a woman in their hearts.

Susan waited until the lesson should have had

time to sink in before she gave the order to take in the light canvas and double reef the topsails. It was for their salvation as well as hers, they realized, and with no thought of mutiny or anything but the subject in hand, the men sprang into the rigging. Susan stepped back on the poop sufficiently far to enable her to command the men on the mizzen in case they should attempt anything overt. It was well that the *Hiram and Susan* carried a large crew, for working with incredible rapidity they had scarcely made things snug when the storm broke upon them.

As the men tumbled down from aloft and in obedience to a gesture from Susan went forward, Mr. Conant came out of the cabin. He, too, had armed himself while below with Mornington's sword and pistols. Four or five hours of sleep had greatly refreshed him and he looked a new man.

"I'll take the deck now, Miss Susan," he began as he reached her side.

Susan nodded to him.

"What sort of a watch did you have?" he asked.

"The men, led by Georgios, came aft and demanded to know where the ship was going and who commanded and other things."

"The insolent whelp!" growled the mate. "What did you do?"

"I refused to answer."

"And then?"

"They made a move toward me and I told them that I would put a bullet into the first man that came nearer, so they went forward, and I have kept them forward of the mainmast except when it was necessary to reef tops'ls."

"By Heaven!" cried the mate. "It was magnificent. I wish I'd been there. You're the very wife for a sailor."

"Why shouldn't I be?" said Susan, smiling faintly, not insensible to his hearty praise. "I was born on the ocean, you know. Now, I'll go below and get some sleep. Call me by rapping on the deck over my head, if you want me. You know my cabin, and remember those men are dangerous."

"I shan't forget it," said the mate grimly. "Good night."

CHAPTER XIX

BLIND AND A FOOL

THE wild motion of the ship in the hard gale raging, for the mate had found it necessary to put the *Hiram and Susan* before the wind and further reduce sail shortly after he took the deck, rendered it impossible to prepare the regular meal at the galley fire. The Spanish cook had managed to boil some coffee, and from this, with the cold remains of the dinner, Susan made a sorry repast. As before she had no appetite, but common sense taught her that she must eat to live.

When she had finished she went over to the door of Mornington's cabin, knocked upon it, inserted the key in the lock and opened it.

"You have had your supper?" she asked.

"Mr. Conant was thoughtful enough to attend to that," was the reply.

"Will you come out into the cabin? I wish to talk with you."

"I should prefer not. There is nothing that we can talk of with profit; no subject that needs discussion between us."

"Will you come out into the cabin?" the girl flamed forth passionately.

"Is this a request or a command?"

"A request, of course."

"In that case, no."

"A command then."

"And from whom?"

"From the woman you—from the master of this ship and your captor," said the girl, checking herself just in time.

"In that case, I presume I have no option."

"None," she replied.

He stepped into the cabin, closed the door of his stateroom and stood before her.

She motioned to the transom.

"Sit down," she said abruptly.

She was trembling so that she could scarcely contain herself and did not trust herself to say more until she could recover in some measure her composure. The woman who had faced the mutinous crew and cowed them was in a state of pitiful nervousness before this single, careless, indifferent and somewhat impertinent young man.

"You are armed?" he began, as he obeyed her gesture.

"I am, of course. Why?"

"That's well," he returned, "for I might take advantage of your defenseless state to—"

Her hands fumbled nervously at the buckle of her belt. She unclasped it, lifted it up and with its cargo of steel and artillery crashed it down upon the table.

"There!" she said, "we stand on equal terms."

"Pardon me, no man stands on equal terms with a woman."

"You are right. I am unarmed now and you are the stronger."

"That also I might dispute, for had I been stronger I should not be in this situation and you in yours."

"What do you mean?"

"I should not have let a woman"—he paused to give due weight to his words, and added slowly—"that I once thought I loved befool me in this way."

"That you once thought?" asked the girl, rising to the snare.

"You have repeated my remark, which, after the experiences of last night, requires neither explanation nor further confirmation, I presume."

"I see—I know," said Susan, "that you do not

—you cannot—you never did care for me—that it was all a pretense on your part."

"Then what was it on yours?" he burst out fiercely.

"I never pretended anything."

"No?" he queried. "And that answer you were to give me on the morrow when I pleaded like a fool for your love? Yours!"

It is not in written words to express the contempt in that pronoun. Susan shrank under its force and then she compelled herself to meet his glance.

"Whatever my feelings were," she said, "they have not changed, and if you really care for that answer—you may have it—now."

"The state of your feelings, madam, is not a matter of deep concern to me now, and as for the answer, I have it in a lost ship and a ruined career, and a heart that you trifled with."

"No, before God, no!" protested the girl. "Can't you understand that I—I had to do it!"

"I understand nothing save that I trusted you with my heart, my honor, and that you blinded me by your beauty and your infernal coquetry."

"I know not the meaning of that word," she interrupted, seizing upon that last phrase. "I have known no women. Their wiles and devices are meaningless to me. I have known few

men save my father, and never one like you. I
would rather have lost my ship than have lost—
than have you think of me as you do, but—"

"Pray, madam, let us end this interview. 'Tis
to no purpose. We are severed, you and I, and
even if you had loved me you would not care to
unite your fortunes with those of a ruined—
broken—dishonored man."

"If I loved you," exclaimed Susan, "these
would only make me love you the more!"

"If?" queried the man.

"And you must hear me," continued the poor
girl, pointedly disregarding his interrogation,
"for my honor and self-respect are at stake, too.
I don't know what other women would do in like
circumstances. Perhaps they would lock their
lips and close their hearts and suffer and die in
silence. Maybe it is unmaidenly of me, like the
dress I wear, but—"

" 'Tis vastly becoming," said the lieutenant,
rising and scanning her from head to heel, with
a slow, supercilious glance.

"Shame! Shame!" cried the girl. "That is
unworthy of you, of the high ideal I have of you.
Look at me! Since you wish to insult me by
your gaze, you shall do it to your fill."

She rose and stood before him with arms out-
stretched in all the slender grace of exquisite

proportion, whose every line was revealed by the sailor's suit she wore. This time in her heroic audacity she did not blush. She was deathly pale, and yet there was a certain exultation in her heart, for she who had been so grievously in error according to him had for the moment put him undeniably in the wrong.

He was a bold man, but he could not sustain the fierce directness of her glance, because his conscience smote him even as her words.

"Madam," he said, bowing very low, "you are right. I can do no more than ask your pardon."

"I grant it," said the girl, sitting down again. "There is nothing I could not forgive you, but you—"

"That's a different matter," he replied, shaking his head.

"Well, whether you forgive me or not, you must hear me."

"Is it another command?"

"It is a request from a woman suffering to a man who was once compassionate."

She attacked him subtly, swiftly, powerfully. From one of his temperament there was but one answer to that appeal.

"At your wish, madam," he said gravely. "I beg you to proceed."

"I am now, as you know, the sole owner of this ship."

"And you must value her highly."

"I value her as nothing compared with honor or love. If I loved a man and a ship stood in the way, I could see her sink with no feeling but that of joy that what parted us was gone, but I am not alone concerned. No one knew it but my father and myself; this ship carries arms for Washington and his men. In one of the chests in the hold there is the latest subsidy from France, a million francs in gold; the cargo belongs to certain merchants of Boston, friends of my father and of my house. I am responsible for these things. When I got a note from the mate, there by the foremast yesterday—"

"That affair of the kerchief? Then you deceived me!"

"It was a ruse," explained the woman piteously. "The mate had made his plans, not I. They depended upon me to secure you. Can't you see how I was torn! You had kissed me in this cabin in the sweetest hour of my life. You had asked me a question, which, but for that note, I would have answered then and as you wished. I loved you then. The confession burned in my soul. But how could I admit my love and then take from you the ship? The note sealed my lips. My heart dragged me one way; my duty to my country, to my friends, to the mate and the men who trusted me, forced me another. What could I do? Has a woman no sense of honor? Should she not be governed by the same principles by which you would regulate your life? We are enemies, not personally, but you belong to the oppressor and I to the oppressed, and the relation is exhibited here and now. What else could I do? Would to God that I might have died! Love and hope and life died in my breast when you passed me by in the cabin last night with bitter words and hateful looks. I love you!"

He started forward at this reckless disclosure of her feelings, but she went on:

"I love you more than sea or heaven. I did not know what it meant before. I don't know all that it means now except that it means suffering and heartbreak."

And she was not the first woman who found only that bitter mingled with the sweet of passion.

"If you look cruelly at me again it will kill me," she continued, throwing restraint to the winds in the turmoil of her feelings. "Can't you see? Don't you understand? See, I am abasing myself before you! I am giving you the answer you have not yet received in spite of all you have said about getting it last night. Try to think for me; try to understand that only the sternest compulsion made me do what I did, and then, if you want me, if you care for this wretched, torn, broken heart of mine, it is yours! Nay, whether you care or not, it is yours! Why should I conceal it? I am not ashamed of it. I can't help it. I love you and only you. You are all I have and—I have lost you!"

Mornington was profoundly moved. The boldness of the wild, passionate avowal shook his previous resolution to the core, and yet he did not give way to his own emotions. Men and women in love, they say, are nine parts fool and one part angel. Usually the nine parts fool crush down the one, but sometimes the one part overbalances the nine. In his case the nine parts were still uppermost and raging.

"You speak of love to me!" he said, lashing himself into crueler and crueler mood as he proceeded, "to me whom you have ruined and dishonored and shamed? You expect me to be treated this way and to give trust and confidence and affection once more; to believe words with which perhaps you would fain mock me again?"

"My God!" prayed the woman, "is it possible that he does not see truth and devotion in all that I say—in all that I am?"

"I see nothing," said the man, "that warrants me in changing my opinion."

It was a falsehood. He knew it was a falsehood as he spoke, but he would not be persuaded.

"And you will not put yourself in my place? You will not see the compulsion upon me? You will not believe that I love you?"

"I put myself no place but where I am. I see nothing. I believe nothing."

"Have pity! Have mercy!"

"Did you have pity on me?"

They were very close together now, the narrow table only between them. She reached over and took his hand.

"Look at me," she cried, crucifying her pride, her dignity, everything in one last appeal to him. "Look at me! You must see that I am truth itself with you."

The Roman centurion could look upon a hideous cross and believe in Divinity there, but this man, blinding his eyes by prejudice and pride, saw nothing. He stared at her coldly for a moment; his eyes plunged ruthlessly through her own swimming vision as a sword strikes the heart.

"Why prolong this interview further?" he said, rising and withdrawing his hand. "We have played our play, you and I, and you have

won and I have lost.   I am a poor loser.   I cannot even congratulate the winner, for whom my
feelings were best not expressed."

"May God forgive you for your words and
deeds!" she said.   "And may He soften your
cruel, ruthless heart!"

She staggered past him into the privacy of her
own room, leaving him standing free and
triumphant in the cabin.   But it was a triumph
in which he took no joy.   He realized as she
turned from him that he had derogated from the
high standard which he set to himself and that
he had acted like a coward and a fool.   He
turned impulsively to her door, knocked upon it,
threw it open.   She was standing in the cabin.

"What do you here?" she asked.

"I have been a fool," he began.

"Ay," said the woman, "you had your chance
for my heart and threw it away."

"Forgive me!" he pleaded, kneeling before
her and stretching out his arms towards her.

She thrust him aside with her hand, she almost
spurned him with her foot.

"God may forgive you," she said, unconsciously using the words of another breaking heart of a
greater woman, though of a lesser love.   "God
may forgive you, but I never can!"

She had been so mocked and humiliated, so

spitefully treated and so outrageously used, that even her overwhelming affection was in abeyance and she rejoiced at the solace to her pride presented by the kneeling figure.

She looked coldly at him a moment, while he stared at her amazed. Was this the woman who had thrown modesty and convention to the winds and pleaded for his love, this young goddess who towered over him and drove him from her with disdain? He rose to his feet awkwardly.

"Now, go to your cabin," she said.

Without another word, he turned and stalked gloomily into his stateroom, she following. With a vicious snap, she turned the key in the lock after him, and he felt that now, indeed, the separation was irrevocable and that she had at last locked him out of her heart.

CHAPTER XX

STORM AND STORM

THE trained sailor will sleep calmly through the greatest accumulation of ordinary and usual noises incident to the motion of his ship. Generally the slightest unusual sound will awaken him instantly. Susan had lain down practically fully dressed, having merely slipped off her coat, waistcoat and shoes when she turned in. In view of the unsettled state of affairs on the ship, it was a wise precaution. Also she had her belt with sword and pistols near at hand.

She was awakened in the middle of the night by a pistol shot and a loud voice calling her by name. A sailor is a creature of instinct largely. He must awake quickly. He must be immediately alive to an emergency. The calls upon him are so sudden that he has no time for consideration. The profound lethargy of sleep must give place to instant action. The cry of alarm had scarcely sounded before she was on her feet, and with the belt in one hand opened the door with the other.

A half dozen steps brought her to the quarterdeck. The storm was at its height. The ship was rolling and pitching tremendously. Everything had been snugged down during the watch; even the top-gallant masts had been struck and the *Hiram and Susan* was laboring along under fore-storm-staysail and a bit of maintopsail. The wild wind shrieked and raved as it tore through the top-hamper. Rain and spray driven by the hurricane swept the decks. At intervals the sky blazed with vivid lightning. Between the flashes the thick darkness graved with mystery fell like a funeral pall. The deep intestine thunder rolled athwart the hidden sky in intermittent peals of tremendous force. The diapason in the clouds had not awakened the woman after the first clap or two, but the sharp pistol shot had.

Into such a scene as that, with all the artillery of heaven in play, in a mad tempest whose force beggars description, the unrulable passions of men strove to match the tumult and strife of nature. One of the lightning flashes disclosed a huddle of men around the mainmast, François in the lead. The wavering light was reflected from the bright blades of bared sheath knives

high upraised as if to strike. Before the group
one of the men lay on the deck groaning. Above
her on the poop towered the gigantic form of the
mate, pistol in hand. Something had happened.
Evidently the men had chosen this unpropitious
moment when even prudence itself would be un-
suspecting, to release François, who had at once
organized a mutiny and was now attempting to
seize the ship. Susan realized it all at once.
The mate had shot one of them and then he had
called for her.

The same lightning flash by which she saw the
men disclosed her to them. Quick to see the advantage of her presence, François, the big boatswain's mate, bellowed out:

"Seize the girl and then he can do nothing."

But the mate saw her at the same time. He
had expected her, but not so quickly, and he had
not calculated upon the adroit movement of the
men. They surged toward her as the roll of the
ship permitted, and Conant perceived instantly
that he must leave his vantage point upon the
high poop and interpose himself between the
woman and her assailants. Disdaining the ladder, he leaped over the low rail and landed on
the quarterdeck, just as the men, whose progress
was naturally slow on the tossing ship, had about
closed with Susan. The girl had time to thrust

a pistol into the mate's hand as he sprang before her.

"Back," cried Conant. "Bring out the lieutenant to help."

A word was sufficient to Susan. She realized that alone the mate could do little. She turned and ran to the cabin again. As she entered she heard the pistol she had given the mate crash once more, then a wild scream and the oaths and curses consequent upon a mighty struggle. She carried the key of the prisoner's stateroom always about her neck. Even in the exigency she was not confused. Her hands found the lock with unerring accuracy. She turned it and the lieutenant himself, who had heard her, threw open the door.

"What is it?" he cried, for he, too, had been awakened by the first shot and had wondered what was happening. Could his men by any chance be struggling to regain the ship?

"Mutiny," said the girl briefly. "Our own crew have released the murderer and are trying to kill the mate. Will you help?"

"A weapon! Give me a weapon."

She handed him the belt with the remaining pistol and the sword. He jerked the one from its sheath, whipped the other from its scabbard, and ran to the door, followed by Susan, now un-

armed and defenseless.   In the exit he hesitated
a moment.   He had been deceived once.   He
might be again, and as he stood waiting for a
lightning flash, staring at the dark mass swaying
and struggling along the deck to leeward, Susan
brushed by him and ran toward the midship line.
As she did so the man at the wheel left his post.
With what feeling of excitement he had clung to
the wheel during the mêlée can scarcely be described.   Now he saw another figure coming
toward him, and instinctively mistaking her for
the enemy, he recklessly abandoned his hold on
the spokes.   The ship gave a violent plunge and
in another moment would have broached to had
not Susan seized the wheel.

Finding himself unpursued the man turned.
A lightning flash revealed the woman.   With an
oath he rushed at her, to be met by another lightning flash in the form of a sword blade that
pierced his throat until the guard smashed
against his upthrown chin. It was Mornington's
skilful arm which had driven home the mighty
blow. He had seen enough in that flash to know
that it was indeed a mutiny and not an attempt
on the part of his own men to take the ship. His
course was clear.

The huddle on deck to leeward was quieter
now.   There was still a writhing movement

about it. The men hung over some dark object, snarling like wolves tearing their prey. Alone he could do nothing against them. With a prayer to God that He might have Susan in His keeping, the lieutenant ran forward with fleeter steps than he had ever compassed in his life before. One of the guards over the fore-hatch had been drawn into the fray aft. The other was waiting and watching not so much the hatch as the struggle on the quarterdeck. Naturally mistaking the approaching figure for one of the *Hiram and Susan's* crew, he called out:

"Have they got him?"

"They have not," said Mornington grimly, and again that swift blade, driven with a force and energy of which one looking only to his slight build would hardly have dreamed him capable, was sheathed in flesh and blood. The man shrieked and fell. As he did so, the other guard detached from the group by the command of the burly boatswain, came running forward. A bullet from Mornington's only pistol met him in full career and he rolled into the lee scuppers dead on the instant.

Without losing a moment, for now there was a swift rush from aft of the men, who had apparently accounted for the mate, Mornington knelt down, drew out the bolt, undid the hasp

and called to his men. They, too, had heard
the pistol shots and the noise. They were all
awake, crowded at the foot of the ladder.

"On deck here, you *Rockinghams,*" he cried,
in a voice heard high above the thunder and the
storm. "Lively, for God's sake!"

Instantly the English sailors came crowding
up the ladder. Scrambling on deck, they found
Mornington in front of it, holding the hatch,
keeping a half dozen men at bay by the brilliancy
of his sword play. The Englishmen had no
weapons, but the fife-rails were handy. Belaying pins and marline spikes were whipped out of
the rails instantly and in a compact body the
British sailors, burning to avenge their treatment
of the night before and to recapture the ship, in-
spired now by the lieutenant's voice and led by
young Merryfield, threw themselves on the pirate
crew—American in name only.

There was a wild, fierce battle upon the slanting deck. In the forefront of the strife raged
the young midshipman. He had had the quickness to pick up the cutlass of the sailor whom
Mornington had killed on guard, and with it he
struck boldly at the big Frenchman, who was in
the lead. The man threw up his left arm and the
keen blade bit to the bone. Mad with rage, before the boy could withdraw his cutlass, he

sprang upon him, seized him by the throat, drove his knife home into the lad's breast and stabbed him again and again in brutal ferocity until Mornington's sword cut him down. And the lieutenant never delivered a blow with a gladder heart or a greater satisfaction than when he sent this villain to his account.

The scene on the deck was one of appalling ferocity. Amid one of the hardest gales that had ever swept across the ocean, with the ship heaving and tossing as a cork in the gigantic seas, the frenzied men battled and struggled and fought with one another like wild beasts. The issue was for a long time doubtful, but presently the mutineers were beaten down and overpowered on every hand. They had sustained a most serious and disheartening loss when Mornington had killed the boatswain. There was neither giving nor taking of quarter, but by and by the battle ceased because the mutineers were either killed, wounded or overwhelmed by main strength and superior resolution.

So soon as he could do so, Mornington, telling Palmer to secure the prisoners that had remained alive, ran aft to the quarterdeck. He found Susan still grasping the wheel, holding the ship on her course in spite of the terrible jerks and jumps which nearly tore the spokes from her hands. Her face in the light of the binnacle lamp was deathly pale. Although the hard gale made the night cold, drops of sweat beaded upon her forehead. In her eyes he could see a look of horror and anxiety unspeakable.

"Are you unhurt?" he cried as he approached her.

"Yes, yes," she answered. "And you? Oh, my God! there's blood upon you," she shrieked, as he came near enough for the faint radiance of the lamp to discover the gory marks upon his shirt.

" 'Tis not my own," he answered grimly. "Aft here, one of you," he roared, "and take the wheel. You must get to the cabin," he continued as one of the seamen relieved the woman. And as he observed she staggered, he caught her by the arm. "And we must have lights."

"There are lanterns in the cabin," she answered. "And I cannot go until I have seen."

Together they entered the cabin. With eager hands he kindled the spare lanterns from that hanging at the bulkhead, which was always kept burning at night. And together they went out upon the deck again. The wind was still rising and the fierce gale almost swept them off their feet. He wondered as he stepped across the deck how human beings could have kept any footing for fighting, much less for anything else, on that tumbling ship.

There were six bodies rolling in a mass to leeward; the man Mornington had killed by the wheel, the Greek, a negro from New Guinea, two sailors and the mate. Some of the English seamen had come aft. Palmer reported that there were three or four unwounded of the crew whom he had lashed and passed below, and that there were a number of dead bodies on the deck forward and several wounded. Two of the seamen bore the body of young Merryfield in their arms. How small and inconsequent he looked! came into Susan's mind as she saw him. Nodding to one of them to take him into the cabin, Mornington bade the others assist him in disentangling the heap against the lee-rail. The man he had struck at the wheel was dead; two had been shot; the Greek had been killed by a slash of the mate's cutlass; another had had his head battered in by the butt of Mr. Conant's pistol. Conant himself was still alive, but senseless and speechless, of course. What a fight he had made before they dragged him down!

Two of the men, by the direction of the lieutenant, carried the mate also into the cabin and laid him by the side of the dead midshipman. By Mornington's orders, the dead pirates were

lifted up and dropped overboard without ceremony. Then he turned to Susan.

"I am going forward now. Will you take the
deck here, and—"

Susan nodded.

"Hurry," she said, "and if there are any
wounded bring them into the cabin."

Besides François, the boatswain, and the two
guards whom he had killed, there were two
others of the mutineers dead around the fore
hatch, their brains having been beaten out with
belaying pins. Five more were severely wounded and incapable of action, and three of the
pirates had been lashed and tumbled below.
There were seven Englishmen, including Mornington, who were fit for duty, although several
of these were slightly hurt. A sad and terrible
ending to the wild adventures of the night!

The attempt of the original crew to seize the
ship would have been completely successful had
it not been for the mate's forethought in releasing Mornington and the skill with which that
young man had used not only his sword but his
wits in bringing to the rescue his own crew.

Casting overboard the bodies of the dead, and
directing the less severely hurt to be taken into
the forecastle, while those more desperately
wounded were sent aft to the çabin, Mornington

soon had some semblance of order restored. Telling Palmer to take charge for the moment and call him instantly in any emergency, he rejoined Susan and together they entered the cabin.

Two of the Americans and the English sailor, with the mate and the midshipman, had been brought there. The ship was rolling so that it had been necessary to lash the helpless men to the transoms or to the stanchions of the table. By Mornington's orders, and at Susan's suggestion, the mate was carried into her own cabin. The English sailor and the two pirates were bestowed in three of the other cabins, of which the *Hiram and Susan* had six.

Like every sea officer of the period, Mornington had a certain skill in a rough and ready sailor-like surgery. He went first to the mate, bared his breast and examined his wounds. The brave American had been stabbed in a half-dozen places. His head had been beaten and bruised by fists and belaying pins. A less strong man would have died long since, but the mate still survived, although his days were evidently numbered. Susan washed the blood and dirt from his face, while the lieutenant bandaged his wounds as best he could and stopped the flow of blood.

"Will he live, think you?" asked the girl.

"No," said the lieutenant shortly, " 'tis impossible."

"He was very good to me," she said softly, tears dropping upon his face.

"Yes," said the lieutenant, "he was a rough man, but a brave one."

"Will he recover consciousness, think you?"

"I cannot tell."

"I should like him to know that I thank him and appreciate what he did."

"You may have your chance. Let us hope so," he returned, too magnanimous now, in the face of swiftly approaching death, to be jealous of her evident interest.

They made the mate as comfortable as they could and then went to the others. Mornington would have spared the woman this, but she insisted that she had a woman's right to such service and that she could help him better than anyone else at his hard task, and in the end she had her way.

One of the mutineers was plainly dying; the other might perhaps recover; the English sailor, too, was in a serious way, but for him, too, there was a glimmer of hope.

"Tell me," said Susan to the dying mutineer, "what possessed you?"

"It was François," gasped the man, "him and the Greek. They told us we could seize the ship —and take her into Algiers and sell the cargo and make away in an open boat, and say we'd been captured by the *Rockingham* and had re-captured the ship—and she had been wrecked, and so on."

"And what were you going to do with me and my men?" asked Mornington sternly.

"Overboard with you," said the man.

"And with this lady?" continued the lieutenant.

"She was to belong to— Don't strike me," he cried weakly, as the lieutenant bent over him with clenched fists.

"The man is dying," said Susan, interposing her hand between the lieutenant and the wretched sufferer.

"The villain!" cried the lieutenant, trembling as he had not trembled during the whole course of the crowded hour, at the ghastly threat implied in the man's words. "Thank God that I was able to come to your assistance!"

"You have saved my life, my honor, everything!" said the girl.

The man in the berth laughed feebly.

"Some of the credit's due to the mate, miss," he gasped out brokenly.

"Don't say anything more," said Susan, wiping the blood from his lips.

"I want to tell it before I die. It's only fair. Perhaps it'll help me."

"Go on, then," said the girl.

"When he jumped forward of you on the quarterdeck, you remember?"

"Yes, yes."

"We made a rush at him. His sword went through one man; he shot a second; his pistol beat down another, and then we closed on him. He jerked a knife out of somebody's hand and stabbed me and then he bore us all across the deck. I don't see how he done it. It wasn't until we got at his back we pulled him down, and then he lay there heavin' and strugglin' and fightin', and we a-strikin' at him. He was a man. God!" he said, "I'd like—"

But what he would like was of no moment, for as he gasped out the word he went to another place where individual likes and dislikes, alas, no longer count.

Susan stared painfully at the figure, silent after that convulsive struggle which marked dissolution.

"He's dead," said Mornington quietly, "come away."

"My God! My God!" exclaimed the girl, suffering herself to be led from the cabin.   "What horror of blood, what suffering, what murder, what loss of life, for one little ship!"

"And for one woman," said the lieutenant solemnly, looking fixedly at her.

CHAPTER XXI

THE ANSWER

GOING from one wounded man to another, Susan got little rest that night. As near as she could judge, it must have been shortly after midnight that the attack occurred. The dawn was soon at hand. The mate's condition was about the same; the English sailor was sinking fast and the other mutineer was just about as he had been. For a long time Susan lingered over the mate. She had succeeded in forcing some spirits and water into his mouth. The flow of blood, she observed, had stopped, and she prayed that he might at least regain consciousness.

To her came Mornington, wet to the skin, haggard and worn not merely with the strain of the night before, but with the burden of a peril of which she had hitherto known nothing. The greeting between them was short, no words being wasted in such an emergency.

"You have slept?" he asked.

"I could not."

"How are the men?"

"Your man is dying. The mate seems a little stronger and the bleeding has stopped. The other man is just the same. You look badly," she said, her heart touched, "you have had no rest."

"It isn't that," he answered, and then he hesitated, wondering whether he would better tell her of their probable peril or not.

"What is it?" she asked, instantly perceiving that something lay back of his reticence. "What has happened?"

"I don't know whether to tell you, or—"

"You must tell me. Think you I have gone through all this to blench or shrink from anything? Is it some new danger that threatens?"

He nodded.

"And what is it?"

"I don't know where we are," he said. "The last time I took an observation we were about fifty leagues from Plymouth. I don't know what course the mate sailed after he got the ship, or whether he took an observation or not."

"He did not," answered Susan. "There was no sun. As to the course, he headed her as near west as the wind would let him, he was on the wind and constantly tacking all day until the gale broke and that was last night at six o'clock. Since then, we've been driving before it, I believe."

"Yes, I should think so from the weather she was making of it. And how fast do you think we might be going?"

"I have known the ship to do eleven knots before the wind. Say, as she is heavily loaded, that she has been doing ten."

"That would be about it, I should judge," returned the lieutenant.

"Well?" said Susan.

"Well," said the other gravely, "the mate's sailing westward has more than been neutralized by our wild dash to the northeast, and—"

"And?"

"I think we are well in the English Channel and being driven toward the coast with every moment."

Susan understood entirely the ominous prospect involved in that simple announcement. Before her rose all the perils of that which a sailor dreads the most—a lee shore!

"Is there nothing to be done?" she asked.

"Nothing but drive on. I never experienced such a hurricane."

"What canvas have you got on the ship?"

"Not a rag. She's driving under bare poles."

"Can't you heave her to?"

"I don't dare."

"We are in God's hands," said Susan.

"Yes," returned the other.

"We must even do our best, I suppose, and—"
But he interrupted her once again.

"That isn't all," he said, now determined to leave nothing untold.

"What more?"

"The ship's leaking badly forward. She almost broached to last night, and had it not been for your quickness she would have gone over on her beam-ends and foundered.. The terrific pounding she has had has opened a butt somewhere or started a seam, and—"

"You mean she's going down?"

"I don't believe she will be afloat in four hours," returned the man solemnly.

"Have you tried the pumps?"

"Yes, but we have only a half dozen men—"

"And the mutineers?"

"There are only three of them. She's making water too fast. It would be useless."

"She rides steadier than she did," said Susan, after a pause.

"That's because of the water that's in her," returned Mornington.

"Is there anything more?" asked the woman.

"Nothing. Isn't that enough?" he added, somewhat bitterly.

"Enough! and more than enough! Oh, think of it, the lives that have been lost, the blood that has been shed, the hearts that have been broken for the possession of this ship, which in a few hours will be as nothing! If we could only see beforehand what we strive for!"

"It is as you say," said the lieutenant, "if we could only see for what we strive it would some· times take the heart out of us. But it is better, after all, to strive than to be supine and indiffer· ent to fate."

"Yes—yes—I suppose so," said the girl wearily. "Meanwhile what are you going to do?"

"Get the boats provisioned, make all ready, bring the wounded men up on deck, and if she founders—"

"The boats would not live a minute in such a sea," said the girl.

"At least," said the lieutenant, "we will die doing our best." And in his simple creed that was a paramount thought. If men must die, it was surely better that they should die doing their best than doing nothing at all—and women, too!

"And if she strikes before she founders?" asked Susan, her mind reverting to the other alternative.

"God help us all!"

"It may be that this will be our last interview alone," began the girl. "I want to say this to you, that I am sorry I drove you away last night when you asked—my forgiveness. I didn't mean it. My feelings—I say it in the presence of death—have not changed. You will believe me now, surely?" she questioned.

"And hear me say, who like yourself am facing death, that never in my heart of hearts have I really doubted you for a single moment. I know that you are true and faithful."

"Appearances were against me," urged the woman.

"I had no right to think of them for a moment and I wish to tell you that I love you as I love life, and liberty, and honor; that my devotion is only equaled by my shame that I have used you so ill; that I chiefly regret the death that seems before us because I cannot prove to you my repentance—and my deep, overmastering, abiding affection for you. We can be nothing to one another now, but I beg your forgiveness and I tell you that I consider you my wife before God and in the sight of Heaven."

"Will you take your answer now?" she asked, thrilling with passion which not even the storm or their peril could shadow or diminish.

"Yes," he said, his heart leaping to meet the question.

"The answer is here," she continued, extending her arms to him, "in my arms and on my lips!"

And there in the cabin, ranged about by the bodies of the dead and dying, upon the storm-tossed, weather-beaten, wounded ship, her vitals filling with that which had upborne her, but which would now soon drag her to destruction, these two clung to one another with kisses long and sweet—to which that which had been before given and received was as nothing.

"At least," said the girl, drawing back a little —but only a little—from her lover's embrace, "I shall not have lived in vain. You love me. Whatever happens, I have had at least one taste of Heaven."

"My dear! My sweet!" he said, releasing her and stooping down and raising her hands to his lips, "I am so unworthy of you that your love fills me with shame. Would God that in some way I could show you how I feel before we die!"

"I want nothing," answered Susan rapturously, "but the memory of this moment to go out with me into the Beyond. Nay, no more," she urged, fondly surrendering herself once again to his ardent embrace, "we have work to do, and—"

"Susan—Miss Hubbell," came thickly from the cabin aft.

It was the voice of the mate. The woman turned instantly and, followed by the officer, entered the cabin. The mate stared up at them perfectly conscious, although terribly weak.

"You are safe?" he asked.

"Thanks to you, yes."

"And yon officer?" he continued bravely. Every word was an agony to him, yet he spoke on. "They had overborne me when he got on deck. But I had sense enough left to know that but for him and his men they would have succeeded."

"Mr. Mate," said Mornington, "I haven't been as agreeable as I might have been to you, and I want to say I am sorry. I saw you fighting like a lion against the whole murdering pack of sea-wolves and I wanted to go to you, but there was Mistress Hubbell to look after, and I knew that her only salvation lay in setting my men on those devils. But I give you my word, sir, if I had consulted my inclination, I would have been fighting by your side. I should have counted it an honor to have fought beside a man like you."

"You done the right thing," said the mate thickly. "Whatever happens, it's the woman must be looked after."

"Yes," said the lieutenant, "it is always the woman who stands first with a true man."

"Miss Susan," said the mate, "I guess I'm under way on my last cruise. Ain't that right, leftenant?"

"I could deceive a less brave man," said the lieutenant, "but not you. You are almost ready to slip your moorings."

"Well," said the mate hoarsely, looking affectionately at poor Susan, "I'm glad if it had to be, that I went fightin' for you. I thought to marry you and take care of you, but it ain't to be. What'll happen to you now?"

"I will take care of her as long as we live," said Mornington.

"That's well," said the mate, "she never loved me, perhaps you—"

"My friend," said Mornington, "you are beyond jealousy now, I take it, and so I will tell you. I love her."

"An' you, Miss Susan? Do you care for him?"

The girl nodded.

"Yes," she whispered through her tears.

"He's a brave man," said Mr. Conant, "although he's a bit quick and free with his tongue. He knows how to use his weapons and his wits, too. She's a rare woman, sir."

"I know that," returned Mornington.

"Shall I tell him?" queried Susan, whispering.

"Yes," said the lieutenant.

"We're all doomed on the ship," said the woman.

"What do you mean?"

"Mr. Mornington thinks that the English shore is under our lee. The worst gale in his experience or mine is blowing."

"The ship seems steadier," said the mate, who had the seaman's quick observance of things.

"Yes, but it's because she's making water fast."

"My God! Then it's strike or founder?"

"In the providence of God," answered Mornington.

"I don't believe," said the mate slowly, after a long pause, "that God's goin' to separate you two." He stopped and thought deeply and then went on. "I ain't well acquainted with Him. I ain't never paid the attention to Him that I'd oughter, but I wouldn't do it if 'twas me," he said at last, after a great effort.

"And if God hears anybody's prayer," said Susan, "I think He would hear yours."

"If 'twas for you, maybe," said the mate.

There was a longer pause.

"When do you think she's liable to founder?" he asked again.

"In a few hours."

"What are you goin' to do with me?"

"Take you up on deck and there are the boats—"

The mate shook his head.

"On deck I want to be. I want to die under the open sky, where I've lived. Now, go and make ready," he said. "You've been too long with me, and I want to be alone."

CHAPTER XXII

SHIPWRECK AND TRIUMPH

GENTLY Mornington led the girl from the cabin. He looked at her, uncertain what to do next.

"Would you lie down?" he asked.

"I could not. I want to go on deck."

"Very well. Hold tight to me."

He brought her a great sea cloak, which she strapped around her. Before she left the cabin they both ate some cold provision and drank some spirits and then she slipped the flask in her jacket pocket. There was some shelter on the quarterdeck from the high rails, and they did not venture on the poop. Life lines had been run across the deck. There were two men at the wheel. One man was lashed against the foremast forward, peering ahead, and the remaining two were at the hatch beneath which the American prisoners lay.

A glance over the side showed Susan the truth

of her lover's words. The ship was perceptibly lower now and her buoyancy had been ex-
changed for a deep and sickening sluggishness.
She had been a dry boat, but now the green seas
came flooding aft in quick succession. The end
would be sooner than they thought. The sky
was heavily overcast and the air was full of mist
and spray. Peering to windward or to leeward
nothing could be seen a cable's length away.

Stowing her safely in the lee of the bulwark
and passing a line around her, Mornington kissed
her, regardless of who might see, and made his
precarious way forward. He stopped when he
reached the fore-hatch. She followed him with
fearful eyes as every roll or wave threatened to
carry him overboard. She saw the hatch open
and the two men descend. Presently from it
straggled a melancholy, wretched procession.
The three captives were released and one glance
told them of their peril. There was no time for
enmities then. The men in the forecastle were
warned, and then, under the leadership of Palmer and the lieutenant, the well men made their
way to the boats. To take off the gripes in the
furious sea then raging was an impossibility. If
the *Hiram and Susan* foundered, they would
have to go down with her. Life preservers were
not in use in those days, and they would have to

depend upon gratings, or hatch covers, or such chance supports, frail and useless indeed in such a sea. There was nothing that humanity could do but wait, and that is the hardest task to which humanity is set.

The lieutenant indicated that each could seek such position and take such measures for his safety when the crisis came as his experience dictated, and then slowly made his way aft to where the woman clung. A little gesture explained what she already perceived, the futility of it all. He stood by her, his arm around her, holding her hand for a few moments, while heart spoke to heart in the silent eloquence of a great passion.

Presently he was conscious of a wild gesture from the man forward, whose hand he could see shaking in the air. He sprang up the poop ladder, realizing as soon as his head rose above the rail the terrific force of the storm, and then he stared ahead and to leeward. There, a short distance away, rose the loom of the land, a range of distant hills of which he could make but little in the mist, but which evidently bespoke nearer shores between him and their crests. It was not to be foundering then. The ship would drive ashore. He scrambled down again and pointed to leeward. Almost the hills could be seen from the deck.

"Land," he cried in the girl's ear, and then summoning three or four who had chosen the quarterdeck for their places of security, he went to the cabin and brought out the three wounded men.

"I want to be carried there," the maté had said, pointing upward to the poop as he was lifted out of the cabin. Although it was dangerous in the extreme, Mornington was willing to humor his fancy. He was laid in the lee of the hatch and they passed a line about him through the ring bolts, knotting it lightly over his breast. The other men were laid on the quarterdeck and the wretched wounded mutineers were brought out from the forecastle in the same way. The men, the well men, that is, had done all that they could for the wounded. They began stripping off their shirts and kicking off their shoes preparatory to a wild struggle with the sea.

"What shall you do?" screamed Susan in the ear of her lover.

"Stay with you."

"Try to save yourself!"

"Not without you."

They held on, staring fearfully through the mist and rain at the shore, which was perceptibly nearer. They were waiting with stilled hearts for the shock. There was a strange eagerness

in everybody's mind.   If it were coming, they
prayed that it might come quickly.   The strain
of waiting was more than humanity could bear.

Susan turned and slipped her disengaged arm
around her lover's neck, drew his face down to
her own and kissed him.   It was as if she had
had a premonition that the moment of farewell
had arrived, for with a shock like an earthquake
the *Hiram and Susan* was whirled against a long
shoal projecting from the shore.   The violent
and sudden stoppage of her wild drive threw
most of those who had not lashed themselves to
the rails or masts to the deck.   The shock snapped
the foremast like a pipe stem; that and the presence of the wind on the weakened main tore the
great spar across below the hounds, and immediately thereafter the mizzen-topmast fell in the
general ruin.   A fourfold block from the top-
sail-halyards struck Mornington, still clasped in
Susan's arms, upon the head and shoulder, and
dashed him down senseless to the deck.   The
woman's scream might almost have been heard
above the roar of the tempest had anyone listened.

Not content with the first awful impact, winds
and waves beat again and again upon the doomed
ship, twisted her about and hurled her farther
up on the shoal.   She rolled over on her beam-

ends at last and became wedged in the sand, while the whole storm-driven Atlantic thundered upon her bilge in mad, terrific assault. Her boats were crushed and torn from their fastenings. Her men were washed hither and thither helplessly. The wounded were drowned in an instant. Some of the strong caught floating bits of wreck and disappeared in the white froth to leeward, fighting for life as they were swept away.

In a moment it seemed that Susan, who had clutched madly at the collar of Mornington's jacket as he fell, and who clung to it with all the tenacity of her affection, was alone upon the ship, save for the dead in the cabins and the dying mate, straining against the rope that secured him to the scuttle. She herself would have gone overboard with the rest had it not been for the timely lashing which Mornington had passed around her. At her belt dangled a sailor's sheath knife. Not for an instant relaxing her grasp on the lieutenant, she drew it with one hand, opened its broad blade with her teeth and then cautiously severed the lashing which bound her to the rail. The lee side of the ship was now well under water. So soon as the lashing was cut Susan fell away slowly down the slanting deck, standing at an angle of perhaps sixty degrees, and brought up against the wheel, as she had calculated. Her marvelous nervous strength stood her in good stead now. With a superhuman exercise of it she drew the prostrate form of her lover up and across it, and there they rested, the woman panting, the man unconscious still.

He was still breathing, she noticed with relief, after a quick and anxious inspection of him, although he had not spoken a word since he had been struck. There was some shelter for the two, since the deck was turned away from the sea, and Susan enjoyed a brief respite. The flask of spirits she had slipped in her jacket before she came on deck stood her in good stead now. She opened it, and tried to force some of its contents between Mornington's shut lips, but with little success. Then she swallowed some of the fiery liquid herself. She had need of all her strength, natural and artificial, and of every stimulant that she could get, for what she proposed to do. She had to work slowly, for she could only use one hand. First she cast off her cloak and pea-jacket and threw aside her waistcoat. Then she kicked off her shoes, thinking swiftly as she did so how glad she was that they were a little too large for her feet and came easily off without unbuckling. From a broken part of the rigging she cut a long piece of line. This she managed painfully to pass around Mornington's shoulders, under his arms and then around her own. She was going to try to swim ashore with him or they would drown together, she resolved. There was no better swimmer on the ship, or on many ships, than this girl. But it was indeed a forlorn hope. If she could only get something to give her some support in that wild, whirling pool of frothing sea to leeward, she might have better chance of success, she knew, but there was nothing within reach. She dared not leave the support afforded her by the wheel until she was ready for the desperate venture.

She looked swiftly forward. There was nothing there. The ship was practically stripped to a gant-line. She put her free hand to her eyes for one brief and fervent prayer and then prepared to slip into the sea, when a voice above her that she knew called her name.

There, at the break of the poop, hanging on the rail, which now stood up like a ladder, was the mate. He had summoned his last vestige of strength and energy to her service and was about to show his devotion in death as he had hoped to show it in life. He had seen her preparations and realized perfectly what she was going to do, and he had come to her aid. How he did it, it is impossible to imagine. He had been practically a dead man five minutes before, yet now he clung to the rail and handed her a grating and she noticed in the midst of her anxiety that his hand was the steadiest thing on the ship. She seized it and with more rope lashed herself to it, giving herself a certain play by which she might keep her head above water. With the same line she also passed a lashing from Mornington to the grating as well.

And now she must go. She looked up once again. The Homeric mate had slipped down along the rail to which he was still clinging. The life had gone out of his face and his eyes were closed in the relaxation which comes after a supreme effort to accomplish a heroic purpose, but he clung there with the instinctive tenacity with which brave men fight off death till the very last. Suddenly his hand was extended. It was very near her, and she caught it with her free hand and kissed it. Mr. Conant opened his eyes, understood, smiled and slipped into the sea.

Upon the instant the woman disengaged herself and the man from their resting place on the wheel and plunged in after. She sank at first like a stone with the velocity of her plunge. When she came up she found herself surrounded by boiling froth and heaving sea, but she struck out madly, desperately, with all the courage of her stout heart and all the vigor of her fresh young arms. Fortunately the ship had finally struck in a little cove and the sea had rolled her about so that there was a comparative protection in her bulk from the wildest violence of the beating surf. Had it not been for that this story would have ended then and there. But as it was, the woman felt that there was a bare possibility that she might win through, and she battled for life and love with a wise head, a strong arm and a stout heart. These will generally win if winning be within the possibilities.

Fortunately the tide was approaching full flood. The onrushing wave would carry her forward and the retreating flow would drag her back, but always she gained a little. The shore, salvation, seemed momentarily nearer. In spite of the grating, the body of her lover was a fearful weight to sustain. Indeed, had it not been for that grating they must both infallibly have perished. After the first roll or two she learned to save her strength. While the wave was carrying her swiftly toward the shore she was inert; but when it began to tear her back toward the deep, then she struck out bravely, fiercely, terribly, and sometimes she gained a few feet.

So the long struggle went on, the human flotsam and jetsam ebbing and flowing with the crashing seas until, her heart beating in her mouth, her strength gone, her courage ebbing away, her hope failing and despair in her soul, her foot accidentally touched the shore. It touched the shore on an incoming wave. She dug her bare feet into the sand—much of her clothing had been torn from her in the contest— and strove to stand up against the mighty backward drag of the undertow. The water gripped her with a thousand arms, whirled her about and forced her seaward, as if some monstrous octopus were constraining her to the deep. But she held on, and as the violence of the ebb spent itself, she staggered a little farther inland, splashing in water up to her shoulders.

The next wave that struck her was a prodigious one, which seized her and tossed her swiftly through the air and far inland. Again she fought the deadly undertow, but this time with more success, and by and by, after moments that seemed hours, she staggered up on the wet sands, drawing after her the inert, helpless load of humanity that she loved, and fell exhausted, fainting, senseless, far above the reach of the highest fling of the angry seas.

She had accomplished the impossible, she realized, ere her senses fled and she sank into oblivion. Whether she had brought more than the dead body of the man she loved ashore or not she could not tell. Her last thought was for him, as her last conscious movement was to reach out her hand and lay it upon his head.

CHAPTER XXIII

KIND HEARTS AND TRUE

How long she lay there she could not tell. There was no sun visible to indicate the hour when she came to her senses. She recovered consciousness slowly, and at first in a deathly sickness that came upon her in the extreme weakness and faintness of her condition she realized nothing of what had happened. But by a strong effort of will she presently regained command of herself, sat up on the sand and looked about her. Her glance fell first on the figure of the lieutenant to whom indeed she was still bound—bound now forever in life, or death, and beyond. She crawled toward him and joyed to find him still alive. Indeed, his eyes were open, but he stared at her unknowing. In spite of the drenching rain which had prevented their clothing from drying as they lay on the sand, his head was burning hot beneath her touch. He was in the grasp of a fever.

Her knife still hung at her belt. She drew it and severed the lashings which bound the two together and which bound them both to the grating. Then she rose painfully and unsteadily to her feet and looked about her. The shore where she had landed appeared lonely and desolate. Beyond the high tide line the sandy beach terminated in some scant shrubbery and a few stunted trees. Farther inland, she could see taller trees and other vegetation, and off to the right, some distance away, a little town, apparently set on a hill. Thither she must go for help.

Having settled that much, she turned and faced the sea again. A half cable's length away lay the wreck of the *Hiram and Susan*. It was disintegrating rapidly under the tremendous beating of the seas. Already the shore was being strewed with casks and bales as the waves broke open the hull and got at the cargo. Here and there human figures lay prostrate upon the sands. Some of them, with horribly lifelike motions, were rolled to and fro in the shallows by the waves. But so far as she could tell, she and the lieutenant were the only living figures on the shore.

Thinking rapidly, she decided promptly what should be done. First, she would move the lieutenant farther away from the sea. The tide was plainly on the ebb now, however, and the waves did not come nearly so far up on the sand. She bent down and tried to lift her lover in her arms. This was a task to which she immediately found herself unequal. She might have compassed it had it not been for the fearful and exhausting struggle she had just gone through in bringing him ashore. She could not carry him, but she could drag him. Somehow or other she managed to get him higher on the beach and in the shelter of a small and stunted tree which sprang from the low shrubbery beyond the sand.

Had she consulted her inclination she would have run to the town at once for succor, but there was a bare possibility of life among those other bodies on the shore, and she must first make sure that none of them needed help. It was a grewsome, horrible task, but it had to be done. She went from one figure to the other and found them all dead. The last one she examined had a strangely familiar look that made her heart beat fast as she approached it. It was the huge body of the mate. He was lying face downward in the sand. He had been driven ashore so hard that he was half buried. Scooping away the sand, she turned him over on his back. With her hands she smoothed the sand from his countenance. He was dead, of course. There was a

little smile on his face and in his hand, tightly
clenched, she noticed a scrap of color. It was a
piece of the American flag. He had fought a
good fight, had Mr. Conant, and he had a right
to lie with his face turned up to God and the
colors of his country in his hand. Susan dragged
his body a little farther along the shore, said a
brief prayer and then turned back to where she
had left Mornington.

As she walked, for the first time she became
conscious of her condition. In her fierce battle
with the waves she had lost all her clothing save
her shirt and trousers and the shirt had been almost torn from her. Among the flotsam and
jetsam lay the sodden jacket of a sailor. She
picked it up and slipped it on, shivering from its
cold and clammy contact as she buttoned it across
her breast. Her hair, not long but thick—she
kept it cut short and wore it generally in man
fashion—had come unbound and hung about her
shoulders like a golden mane. With a stray
piece of line clinging to a bit of spar she tied it
roughly together and then, barefooted as she
was, went toward the tree in the hollow where
she had laid her lover.

When she stopped by the tree and looked for
him he was not there. What could have happened? It was impossible that he could have

recovered sufficiently to have gone away unaided. Who had taken him from her? She had saved his life after such a struggle as the uninitiate could scarcely even dream of. He was hers by every right of God or man, and now he was gone. She felt as a mother would feel who had been deprived of her child. Half of the passion with which a woman loves is maternal. This man was hers, and he had been taken away. She could have screamed aloud in agony, but restrained herself to consider what she should do next.

She stood thinking and staring. As she did so, her eye caught a glimpse of a cart being driven along what appeared to be a road inland. Perhaps he was there. It was moving rapidly and she realized at once that she could not overtake it. Nevertheless she determined to follow in its direction. She had not taken ten steps through the undergrowth until she came upon a road. Marching down it was a squad of men, coastguards, evidently, although of course she knew nothing of that. They were a rough, hardy-looking set and they were coming rapidly toward her. She ran to them at once.

"The man under the tree yonder!" she panted.

"Keep cool, my lad," said the leader, who seemed to be a sergeant, "we've got him."

"What are you doing with him? Where are you taking him?"

"To the horspital at Weymouth! What is he to you?"

"I lo—" She stopped suddenly. Some instinct made her realize that concealment was the safest plan. "I fetched him ashore from the wreck yonder," she answered after a momentary reflection.

"That was well done," said the older man approvingly. "What ship is yon?"

"The *Hiram and Susan* of Boston."

"A Yankee ship?"

"Yes."

"But that man had the coat of an English officer on."

"He is an English officer. He captured the ship and was in command when it drove ashore."

"Are you an English boy?"

"No, I am an American," said Susan, who was too proud to deny her nationality under any circumstances.

The sergeant whistled softly.

"American, eh! Well, you'll find plenty of your countrymen in the jail at Weymouth."

"You're not going to take me to the jail?" exclaimed the poor woman, dismayed beyond measure at the prospect.

"Where else?" asked the sergeant, surprised. "You're a prisoner of war, I take it, ain't ye?"

"But the ship was wrecked."

"That don't change things. You're an American. This is England. The only place for Americans in England is in prison."

"But I want to go with Mr. Mornington."

"Is that his name? I don't see how it can be done," said the sergeant. "You see, he's an English officer and I've sent him to the horspital —and you go to the prison."

"But," began Susan, terrified at this new development.

"There's no 'buts' about it. I've wasted enough time talkin' to you. Lads, there's fat pickin's down there and maybe there's some more Americans to be took up. Did any more of you get ashore?"

"Not that I know of. I think he and I are the only ones left alive."

"And what was you on her?" asked the sergeant, "cabin boy?"

"I was—" answered Susan, and then she stopped again. The absurdity of proclaiming herself the owner of the ship was apparent. "I was a passenger," she said.

"Well, it's all the same. Higgins, you take this boy back to Weymouth and deliver him to

Major Weggard.   I'll see that your share of the salvage is saved for you."

"Come along, boy," said the coastguard thus designated, rather ruefully, evidently doubtful of his superior's promise of fair play.

There was nothing to do but to obey, and Susan, accompanied by her captor, marched up the road in the wake of the wagon which had carried Mornington.   She had this consolation, she thought drearily, that they were at least going in the same direction.

Never was there a woman in more melancholy situation.   To her own wretched circumstances were added the maddening doubt and uncertainty as to the condition of Mornington.   That he had been recognized as a British officer would, she knew, insure him careful treatment and every attention, but she would not be there.   Others would do for him what she would fain have done herself.   He would be free and she would be a prisoner.   They were parted.   She could not bear it.

As they marched wearily along the road they met constantly enlarging groups of townspeople who had heard of the wreck and were coming out for the treasure-trove of the shore.   To some of the more important of these Susan's companion explained the situation briefly.

It was several miles into Weymouth, and by the time they reached the prison, which stood on the outskirts of the town, and was indeed only a large stockade especially erected for the care of American prisoners, Susan was almost exhausted. Her bare feet were cut and bleeding. She could scarcely drag one weary leg after the other. Indeed, so pitiable was her condition that her guard would have assisted her had she permitted it, but she kept resolutely away from him, fearful that by closer contact he might discern that she was a woman, the thing she was determined now to conceal at all hazards.

There was a lieutenant in charge of the guard at the gate of the stockade, and to him the coast-guard delivered the prisoner. Major Weggard, the commandant of the prison, was busy, and the lieutenant did not trouble himself to acquaint his superior with so trifling a fact as the arrival of another American. He entered the name of the newcomer, which Susan gave as Hiram Hubbell, in the registry, passed him through the gate and directed one of the warders to put him in one of the least crowded of the pens—they were little more than that—in which the Americans were confined.

After much passing through gates and pas-

KIND HEARTS AND TRUE

sages, Susan found herself thrust into a small enclosure uncomfortably filled with perhaps five hundred men. Anything which broke the monotony of an existence which had no diversions whatever was welcome, and the Americans crowded around her, asking her story. One or two of them pressed close against her. The roughest among them contemplated a little horseplay as an initiation to the noble army of captives. In the scuffle her jacket was torn open and the nearest man sprang back with an exclamation of surprise.

"Mates," he cried, "this is no lad. It's a woman."

"A woman!" yelled another man. "So it is!" he shouted enthusiastically.

"By gad!" cried another, "it's the first female I've seen for a year and a half."

"Give us a kiss, lass, all around," said a third.

The frightened girl was at once surrounded by a tumultuous mob, rough, rude, boisterous, bad-mannered, but not bad-humored. She shrank back against the stockade, her hands drawing together the jacket and shirt over her bosom, her face deathly pale.

"For pity's sake!" she cried, "if you are true men, hear me!"

"Pipe down there!" roared one of the men

nearest to her. "The gal is goin' to make a speech. Give her a chance."

The point where she stood was a little raised above the ordinary level of the enclosure and the stockade had there been carried over a little hillock, so that she was plainly visible to most of those confined therein.

"I am a woman," she began nervously—thé remark being greeted with enthusiastic and ironic cheers which almost rendered her speechless— "my name is Hubbell."

"I know that name," shouted a big, burly man on the outskirts of the crowd, and as he spoke he began to bore his way in toward the interior.

"Thank you. Ten days ago I was on my father's ship and mine, the *Hiram and Susan*, bound from Bordeaux to Boston."

"I know the ship, too," roared the same deep voice of the previous speaker, and at the sound of it Susan thanked God and took courage.

"We were captured by an English frigate and driven ashore in the gale now raging. I managed to save myself, and here I am, a prisoner like yourselves, and at your mercy. If there are true Americans here, I call upon them for protection. I love my country and my flag as you do, and I have suffered for it as much as any," she went on swiftly. "Shall I not have kindness and protection at your hands?"

"That you shall," cried the man who had spoken twice before, now gaining her side. "Shipmates," he called out in his deep, powerful voice, "and soldiers!"—for there were men from both branches of the service among that group— "the lady tells the truth. I sailed one cruise under Captain Hiram Hubbell about ten years ago, and he had his little gal with him, and if I know anything about faces, this was her. We're going to help her and take care of her like true-hearted seamen, and soldiers, too," he added as an after-thought—he evidently thought little of the military. "There don't never a woman ask help of an American sailor that she don't get it. Am I right, mates?"

"Right you are!" came in a roar from the crowd.

"Three cheers for Bob Young and the lady!" cried another.

The men yelled like maniacs.

"Thank you. God bless you!" cried Susan, tears streaming down her face at this manifestation of goodwill and affection. And then she did what she had never done before in her life, unless you count those moments on the sand. She slipped quietly down upon the ground at the foot of the stockade in a dead faint.

"Back now, all of you," said Young, an oldish man, who had been a boatswain on a man-of-war when captured. "Two or three of you old sea-dogs keep the rest away from the lady, and where's some of that rum we got last night?"

Some little trading had been allowed the prisoners, and their own handiwork, in the shape of trinkets, wood carvings and such like, was often responsible for a surreptitious bottle of spirits smuggled in, and for other delicacies added to the hard prison fare. The liquor was forthcoming at once and some of it was poured down the girl's throat. Water was brought and presently, to the great delight of the worthy seaman and his eager mates bending over her, she recovered consciousness.

"What you need now," said Young, whose former rank not less than his personal prowess gave him a certain pre-eminence among the rest, "is food and clothing."

"A dress! I want a dress!" said Susan faintly.

"We'll see about getting that presently," continued the man, "but first you must have something to eat."

The prisoners cooked their own food, and it

was near the noon hour, so that a rude, but to
the exhausted, famished woman, a savory mess
of stewed meat and vegetables was soon brought
to her. Much refreshed by the simple meal, she
essayed to get up on her feet, becoming conscious
as she did so how torn and lacerated they were.
With a sob of pain, she sank back to a sitting position.

"Poor little gal!" said the boatswain compas-
sionately. "Now, miss, if you'll allow me.
I've got children of my own back in God's country and some of them is females like yourself.
Water here," he cried, "and rags."

Some of the men fetched water. Others in
default of anything better tore the shirts off their
backs and handed them to the boatswain. Very
tenderly he washed the torn and bruised feet of
the girl and then bound them up with such rags
as he could get.

"Now, mates," he said, after Susan had gratefully thanked him, "we've got to do something
for this lady. I votes we call on the officer of
the guard."

"Good for you, Bob! We'll back you up,"
came from one and another, and then, leaving
Susan alone, the whole mass surged over to the
gate yelling and shouting for the governor. They
were an unruly lot, these Americans, and certain

privileges were therefore allowed them. It was an open secret that if they were not treated with some consideration they would rise and could only be subdued after horrible bloodshed. They were chafing against confinement, especially as rumors had reached them that the war was practically over and that peace had almost been concluded. Consequently the warders and guards paid more attention to their united demands than they otherwise would.

The mob of prisoners yelling and beating upon the gate speedily brought the lieutenant in command of the guard to the tower that overlooked the stockade.

"What do you want? What are you making all this row for?" he exclaimed gruffly.

"You've put a woman in here by mistake."

"Well, you ought to be glad of that," remarked the young officer cynically.

"Look here," said Young sternly, "you're making another mistake. This is a lady."

"A lady, eh?" smirked the youngster. "Let's have a look at her."

"You'll take my word for it," said the boatswain. "And she's got to be took out of here and treated decent, or we'll break loose and raise hell, and you know what that means."

The lieutenant looked down at the mob of

flushed and angry faces and concluded that discretion was the better part of valor.

"Oh, well," he said, "bring her along. Perhaps she'll amuse me."

"You villain!" cried Young, shaking his fist.
"If you hurt a hair of her head, as there's a God
above me, you'll pay for it."

"You dog!" cried the lieutenant, whipping out
his pistol. "Dare you speak so to me?"

"I do," said Young, "and I mean it."

"An' if he ain't enough, here's me," cried another man.

"And me, too!"

"We'll all do it. Put up that popgun," cried
still another voice out of the tumult. "And
if you hurts a hair of Bob Young's head,
there's six hundred of us 'll do for you when
we get out."

The men snarled and surged and raged like
angry beasts, and the lieutenant shrank back, appalled, from such a display.

"I mean no harm to the wench, you fools," he
said at last when he could be heard.

"Lady!" roared Young.

"Lady! Damn you!" yelled the rest.

"Lady, then," assented the now thoroughly
cowed officer. "Now get back from the stockade and one of you—you're the leader," he point-

ed to Young, "bring her out here. Get back, I say. I'll not open the gate until you've scattered and, mind you, I'll have troops under arms when they open. If there's the slightest disturbance you'll be fired on."

With derisive yells and calls, the men, urged thereto by Young and the older seamen, slowly and reluctantly ebbed backward and scattered about the enclosure. The boatswain walked over to where Susan sat, a startled, frightened listener to it all, and picking her up in his arms as if she were a baby, carried her to the gate of the stockade. It was thrown sharply back, and in front of it, through the opening, could be seen a cannon, backed by a squad of soldiers, muskets presented; a linstock blazed in the hands of the cannoneer. Behind the ranks stood the lieutenant in safety. The boatswain with his precious burden stalked through the gate.

"Put her down. Can't she walk?" asked the lieutenant.

"She cannot," answered the man. "I'm going to carry her where she's to be taken."

"Close round him, a squad of you," the officer ordered as the gates were shut, "and take her over to the hospital."

The hospital was a rude, boarded structure, hastily erected for the sick soldiers of the guard, not for the ill prisoners, who were forced to shift for themselves.

"Shall we put her in the common ward, sir?" asked the sergeant in command of his superior.

"There's no one in the officers' section, I believe. Put her in there. I'll send the doctor over to look after her."

Unwilling to relinquish his charge for a single moment, the seaman carried the girl into the room set apart for the officers, which, as the lieutenant had said, was vacant, laid her carefully down on one of the camp beds which furnished it, covered her over with a blanket, and shook her by the hand.

"We'll look after you," he said. "They won't dare to do anything to you."

"You have been very good to me," she answered, "and I shall remember your name if I ever get out of this place. Young, isn't it?"

"Bob Young, at your service, miss," said the man, turning away. He did not dare to look at the tears in poor Susan's eyes.

CHAPTER XXIV

A BITTER AWAKENING

A WEEK elapsed before Susan was able to get up. The cumulative experiences of the crowded hours through which she had lived since the moment she got the mate's note had been too much for her, and even her vigorous and healthy nature had given way under the tremendous strains to which she had subjected it. For several days after her release from the prison she had been very ill and at times unconscious. The attention of the regimental surgeon had been accorded her in the fullest measure; a respectable woman, the wife of one of the sergeants, had been secured to nurse her, and everything had been done for her that experience and ability could dictate.

The fourth day of her stay in the hospital she had fallen into a deep sleep from which the surgeon would not permit her to be aroused, although a visitor had been most anxious to have the privilege of speaking with her. His business was of such a pressing nature, however, that he was unable to wait even the few hours that might elapse before she awakened. He would not have gone at all, no matter what might have summoned him, had not the surgeon assured Mornington that this sleep was certainly the beginning of recovery which in the case of a patient of so vigorous a constitution as Susan possessed would probably be very rapid.

His prognostications were fulfilled by the event, for Susan woke from the long sleep in her right mind, with the fever broken. She had babbled of Mornington throughout her illness, in which she had gone over many of the most terrible scenes of the tremendous drama in which they two had played a part, and her first question was for him. It happened that the surgeon was present when she awakened. She looked at him steadily for a few moments, his face being totally unfamiliar to her, and indeed for some time she could scarcely get her bearings and realize where she was.

"It's all right, madam," said the surgeon reassuringly, noting the bewilderment in the blue eyes. "You'll know all about it presently. Don't trouble yourself to think too hard. The less you think now, the sooner you'll know more later."

"I know now," said Susan softly, "the ship was wrecked and I brought him ashore."

"Just so, just so," continued the doctor, who had heard what the coastguard and Mornington could tell him of the story, although, indeed, Mornington had not learned the important part of it, that which concerned his own rescue and how it had been effected, until catching a suggestion from the chance word of the doctor, he had sent for the sergeant of the coastguard and had extracted from him all that Susan had told him at the meeting on the ocean road.

"I know all about it," said the doctor.

"But what has become of him?"

The physician hesitated.

"I must know!" cried the girl. With a sudden access of strength she literally raised herself up on her arm. "'Where is he? Not dead?'" Her voice rang high in the room with all the power of health and strength, with all the force of fear and longing, with all the sweetness of passion and devotion.

"Lie down instantly," commanded the doctor, bending over her.

"But tell me! Tell me!" pleaded Susan, sinking back under his gentle pressure.

"He is well, I say, perfectly well."

"Thank God for that! They took him away

from me on the road and I had brought him ashore. He was mine."

"I know, I know," said the surgeon. "Compose yourself, pray, my child. He was here this morning, and—"

"Here!" exclaimed Susan. "Where is he now?" Her heart leaped at the thought that he might be near her and that she might see him in a moment. "Oh, bring him to me!" she pleaded. "I want him so much! That will make me well as nothing else can."

"My dear girl," said the surgeon, an elderly man, deeply affected by her frank yet piteous appeal, "he is not here."

"But he will come back to-day, in a short time?"

"He has gone to London."

"Gone!" whispered Susan, "and without a word to me! Did not he even ask to see me?" she faltered.

"He came in here this morning early and bent over your bed."

"Why was I not awakened?"

"I forbade it."

"It was cruel of you—but you could not know."

"It was the first natural sleep that you had had since you came here. I could not risk waking you up even for, ah—Mr. Mornington."

"And he could not wait until I was awake?"

"His business, he said, was very urgent. He could not stay a moment. Indeed, the sight of you seemed to make him the more anxious to get away."

Susan closed her eyes and for the moment the doctor thought she had fainted, until she waved away the cordial with which he approached her lips.

"No," she said, "nothing now!"

"But you must take this," urged the physician. "It's my business to get you well and strong again as soon as possible."

"That I may go back to the stockade?" said the girl, accepting the draught. "Very well, I shall do whatever you say, and then—the prison. That is all that is left for me. Everything has gone from me—ship—father—love!"

The doctor did not know what to say to this. He patted her gently on the shoulder.

"Now don't talk like that," he urged. "For such a fine, handsome lass there will be plenty of brave and gallant lads from whom she may take her choice, and as for the prison, I'm thinking that the war is about over and you will soon be free. And there are other ships upon the sea."

"Not for me!" returned poor Susan. "He was here. He might have stayed. He has gone away!"

"But he's coming back," said the doctor. "He told me to tell you that he'd be back just as soon as he could; that he wouldn't spare himself or his horses on his journey, and that as soon as he had concluded his business you would see him again."

"I suppose so," answered the girl listlessly, for the words gave her little comfort in the face of his absence. They contained just such an indefinite promise as anybody might have made lightly not meaning to keep it. "How did he look?" she asked at last.

"Badly," replied the surgeon. "Indeed, though I am not his medical man, I ventured to try to dissuade him from going away. His shoulder had been broken. He had received a tremendous blow on the side of the head apparently, and although there was no fracture of the skull, yet he must have come perilously near it."

"Think you he will suffer from going out so soon?"

"I hope not," returned the other. "He's young and strong and healthy, and if he doesn't get cold and isn't reckless—"

"I never knew him to be prudent," said the girl, for the moment thought of her own desolate abandonment swallowed up in concern for her lover.

"Now, don't worry about that," said the surgeon. "You've difficulties and troubles enough of your own without taking anybody else's. And if you only do what I say and make the effort, we'll have you on your feet in no time. When he comes back you'll be able to see him clothed and in your right mind, I trust."

He nodded kindly to her, called the nurse, gave her some directions and turned and went about his other duties.

Declining any attentions which the woman, who had become much interested in her, would have proffered, and indicating her desire to be left alone, Susan gave herself over a prey to melancholy and wretched thought. This was the man for whom she had periled her life. This was he whom she had snatched from the ravening maw of the sea by such an exercise of skill, determination and courage, to say nothing of the expenditure of bodily vigor and strength, as no woman on earth could have matched. For him she had tramped barefooted and bleeding across the rocky road. For him she had endured insults and mockery and shame. For him she had suffered so she would fain have died. And it all meant so little to him! He had come there where she lay asleep, sick, weary, alone, and had gone away with a message that he would return. He might not love her—what he vowed upon the sea he might forswear upon the shore; what he believed in the cabin he might reject in the hall —but gratitude, common gratitude, should have bound him to more than that hasty glance, that careless word of farewell and that idle promise of speedy return.

True, he had business in London. Business! she thought scornfully. What business on earth would have taken her from him at such a time? Thrones might rock and perish; dynasties might rise and fall; fortunes might hang in the balance, she would not have given them a thought had he lain upon the bed of pain and had she bent over him. She raged fiercely and bitterly against his desertion. All the fire and impetuosity of her nature resented it. She was torn by conflicting passions. And ever and again across the turmoil and tempest in her soul, would rise the picture of him wounded, battered, broken, bruised and torn.

It must be business of a most engrossing nature, leaving herself entirely out of count, she thought bitterly, that would force a man to ride away on horseback to London town under such conditions. What could that business be? Men would not usually so far inconvenience themselves unless one or the other of two motives influenced them, money or a woman! He had never manifested the least anxiety or made any reference to his financial condition, neither had he to any other woman for that matter, but that did not count. Instantly there flashed into her mind that the other cause was the mainspring of his action. She forgot for the moment the utter unreasonableness of her surmise. She forgot his look in the cabin, the words he had whispered, the kisses he had pressed upon her lips. She forgot everything but that he had gone away and possibly to some other woman or on some other woman's errand.

And then, in deep abasement, she thought, Why not? What was she? What had she to offer such a man as he? On the ship, surrounded by men, it was all very different. She had a place then, and would have, in any man's respect. She could do things on the ship! The sea was her element! Out of her environment she was nothing. Probably he was thinking about her boy's clothes with amused contempt now that he was ashore where he could see other women.

And he had said he would come back! Yes, that was evidently to keep her quiet. He would never come back.

She turned on the pillow and because she was so weak and feeble and had gone through so much and was so heartbroken, she sobbed herself to sleep again.

CHAPTER XXV

A REJECTED ADDRESS

THREE days after Susan was much better. She was, in fact, dressed and sitting up in a chair near the window. Better in body, that is, not in mind. After that bitter hour of self-communion, when her lover's abandonment of her had been borne home to her, she had awakened to a stern resolution. She would get well that she might leave the hospital and go out of his life. Since he had deserted her, he need not expect to find her on that problematic return of his. She would bend all her energies to recover her bodily vigor. There was no use wasting any time on her heart. That was dead and a dead heart such as hers admitted of no resurrection. She was a very energetic woman on occasion and she amazed the doctor by the rapidity of her recovery.

She had not yet left the room, but she would soon be ready for departure. She sat by the window wondering what would be her destination and what would happen to her out in the world, which looked bright and fair to her and which she had always regarded smilingly until the disasters of the past fortnight.

She was dressed in some loose and comfortable garments which had been fashioned for her by the sergeant's wife, who had become her faithful and devoted adherent. Her hair had been cut short during her illness and what was left clung in bright curls about her head, an unfamiliar fashion then, but one doubly picturesque and beautiful for that. Faint color had come back to her cheek and all her former beauty, softened, chastened by sorrow and suffering, but more striking than ever, was in evidence.

She had not been left alone since the first day she could get up. The lieutenant had called upon her several times and endeavored to smirk his way into her good graces. Major Weggard, an officer who had risen from the humblest walk and who lacked the instincts and habits of his present station, had also made desperate advances to her, apparently with a view to ingratiating himself in her affections. Totally without experience and thinking and caring nothing for men, all her affections following that one man who had gone away, she had not realized the purport of these and other similar attentions from the lieutenant, the major commanding and some of the other officers of the camp. A helpless, penniless American woman, a prisoner dependent upon the bounty of her captors for the very clothes she wore, completely at their mercy, was fair game for any unprincipled man under such conditions, and when the woman in question was dowered with glorious and resplendent beauty, the incentive to effect her conquest was overpowering.

From the window in the hospital she had a view of the parade. She was listlessly looking out, without thinking of what she saw, when she became aware that the stout, beefy figure of the major, resplendent in full regimentals—his habit usually was a somewhat untidy one—was coming toward the hospital. A moment after the door was opened and the burly major stalked in, removed his hat, smiled at her and without asking her permission—indeed, why should he stand upon ceremony with a woman so circumstanced? —drew a chair up to her and sat down.

His chair was so close to her own that Susan looked at him in amazement, amazement greatly increased when he reached over and took her hand. She was positively too astonished to struggle.

"My dear," he began, with a leer of gross familiarity, "the doctor says you're about ready to leave these quarters, and—"

"Will you let go my hand, sir?" she cried, as soon as she could get her breath.

"Of course not," said the major. "Why should I? I hope to hold it longer and more tenderly later on."

Ordinarily Susan would have been perhaps a fair physical match for the stout, wheezy, bloated, elderly soldier, but after what she had gone through she was still terribly weak. She struggled faintly to draw her hand away, but without success.

"Please, I beg of you," she began, "release my hand."

"Never," said the major gallantly. "A gentleman never lets go of a lady's hand once he's got it."

"What do you know about the actions of a gentleman?" flashed the girl, whose wit was in no way impaired by her physical weakness.

"About as much as you do about the actions of a lady," returned the major, who was quick at that sort of repartee.

"If you do not instantly let go of my hand," said Susan, "and move your chair, I'll scream for help, if it kills me."

"Well, you can scream as loud as you want

to," was the reply; "everybody around here is under my orders, including you."

"Do your orders give you the right to insult helpless prisoners—women?"

"They give me the right to do whatever I please," continued the other sulkily.

He still retained his hold on her hand. After the first moment or two Susan had realized the futility of the struggle, but she was a resourceful young woman. Her neckerchief was held together at her breast by a common brooch, which Mrs. Fisher, the nurse, had lent her. Before the major could realize what he was doing she had unpinned it quietly with her free hand, and instantly she got it loose she jabbed the point into the back of his own coarse red hand. With a howl of pain he dropped her hand. Then he rose and stood over her wrathfully, while she coolly replaced the pin.

"This'll get you into trouble, miss. I came here on a pacific errand, to treat you nicely, you little baggage," he began, but as he proceeded further he realized that this was no way to accomplish the end he had set before himself, and so he perforce quieted down a little. "I meant no harm, girl. I should think you'd be honored by the attentions of a British officer."

"I have only known one British officer," said

Susan, "and he was so different from you that I scarce think you belong in the same category."

"You mean that sailor? Well, you needn't pin your affections to him," sneered the major coarsely, "he's gone and left you and there's better men to take his place. Look at me, my dear," he said, tapping himself approvingly on the breast.

"His place!" exclaimed Susan in bewildered amazement, fortunately not at all comprehending the man's disgraceful allusion.

"Certainly," insinuated the major. "Weren't you alone on the ship with him?"

"I was, but—"

"Well, wait a minute. Let me explain it to you. Now, you're a prisoner of war. You've been once in the stockade and you know what sort of insults and rough treatment you're likely to get there," went on the commandant, who had not heard, for the lieutenant had carefully refrained from telling him how Susan had come to be taken to the hospital and how her compatriots really had treated her. "I've got no place to send you but back there with five hundred men" —which was a lie and distinctly contrary to his orders, but in the game he was playing he did not hesitate a minute at so inconsiderable a thing as an untruth—"I've got no option," he went on, overreaching himself, "but as soon as you're well to send you back there. It's my duty and of course, being a soldier, I've got to do it."

"Why," asked Susan, "all this discussion with me of your duty?"

"Because," said the major, leering with what he considered to be an ingratiating smile, "there might be a way out of it. If a man has to choose 'twixt love and duty, he generally chooses love."

"Your kind does probably," said Susan, "but what has that got to do with it?"

"Well, you see, my girl, I'm in love with you, and—"

"You in love with me!" cried Susan. "Why, it's preposterous!"

"Yes, ain't it? I will admit that for a man of my position to pay attention to a woman of yours might strike people that way, but—"

"I don't mean it that way," said Susan.

"Well, however you mean it," went on the major, "the fact's the same. I can offer you a home and every comfort and good clothes."

"Do you mean to say you want to marry me?"

"Marry you! Good Lord!" cried the major, "what do you think I am?"

Susan stared at him still uncomprehending for the moment, and then as the hideous nature of his proposal dawned upon her, her face flamed.

She rose to her feet and anger lent her some of the strength which had wasted away.

"And what do you think I am?" she asked, a little smile upon her face.

"That's what I said," remarked the major, utterly misreading the signs of the times and perhaps seeing in her flushed face an acquiescence utterly foreign to it.

"And you really wish to know?"

"I do."

"I think you are the veriest blackguard left unhung!" said Susan. "I think you are a brute, a villain and more than that, a fool, and lest my words do not convey my mind to your besotted brain, let me demonstrate as nearly as actions can the ineffable nature of my contempt for you!"

She reached over—she had gradually approached him as she spoke and was near him now—and struck him in the face with her hand. It was not a gentle tap, for she delivered the blow with all the strength that remained in her body, backed by a mind and temper so outraged and shocked that for the moment she was completely her physical self again. It was excessively unladylike, doubtless, and a weaker vessel than the poor girl would never have thought of such a thing. It was, in fact, manlike, but Susan had

been reared among men and had unconsciously
perhaps acquired their way of resenting an insult
rather than the usual feminine practice.

The blow made the doughty major's head
fairly ring. For the moment he shrank back,
appalled before this terrific display of passion.
He looked up at her, as she towered over him,
in bewildered amazement. He had expected
resistance. He had not anticipated that the
woman would come to his heel at a call. He
supposed that, like most of the sex with whom
he had been brought in contact, the object of his
attentions would play for a higher bid, and he
was prepared to go to the limit of his capacities.

"You come here to me," said Susan, with with-
ering scorn in voice and bearing, "a prisoner, a
single woman, weak, helpless, ill—"

"Good Lord!" gasped the major to himself,
"if she can hit like that when she's ill, thank God
I didn't tackle her when she was well."

"With every claim," continued the woman
hotly, "that could appeal to an honorable man
for protection, and you insult me with an offer
like that! Love you, associate myself with you
in any way, I would rather tear my throat open
with my own hand or starve myself to death!"

She stepped closer to him again, where he had
shrunk back, and as before he gave way, for his

was a slow mind, and he had not yet awakened to the consciousness of his power and her helplessness. In moral courage he was no match for her, and for the moment he was cowed by the display of her passion.

"I would have you know," she continued relentlessly, "that I love a man, a gentleman. You don't know what the sentiment is that you degrade by calling by that name."

"He's gone away," said the major, at last finding his tongue.

"I don't care whether he has or not. He will return, anyway," said the girl bravely, although the conclusion was a lame one.

"Yes, yes, I suppose so," sneered the major. "They always come back to their cast-offs, don't they? Well, he won't find you as he left you."

"He'll find me that way or else dead!"

"Do you hear me?" cried the major, at last roused to a fury. He stepped near to her, grasped her by the arm and shook her as a cat shakes a mouse. "Do you understand me? "You'll come with me as I choose, and get down on your knees and thank God for the chance, or you'll go back to the stockade, with all its ruffians."

"They are Americans there," said the girl. "They treated me like true men once and they'll do it again. And let me tell you, if a hair of my head is harmed by you or anyone, they'll tear your heart out when they get free. They'll not forget."

The major had an uneasy feeling that there was truth in that assertion, but he was too angry to regard it now.

"That for your threats!" he cried. "Back you go to them, and, by the Lord, you won't go as you came out either!" He stepped closer to her as he spoke, released her arm, threw his arms around her waist and drew her to him.

She threw up her hands into his face and struggled vainly to push him away. Fear lent her strength, loathing and hatred nerved her arm, the resolution that comes to a woman battling for her modesty gave her courage. She felt that if she once permitted his lips to touch her she would be ineffably contaminated and would lose even the right to think of Mornington. But the unequal struggle could not last. Already the major could feel her droop in his arms. He relaxed his efforts a little, as if to prolong the agony, and laughed.

CHAPTER XXVI

RESCUE

SUSAN shuddered in horror, her soul rising in loathing of this man. In a moment it would be all over. She was helpless. Mornington had deserted her. Her lover had gone away. He had not come back as he had promised. She had fought and she had failed. God help her!

In the intensity of the struggle neither of them was aware of an opened door, a sharp exclamation of surprise, followed by the swift rush of hasty steps across the room. The first notice that the major had that his program was to suffer interruption was an iron grasp on his shoulder. Amazed, he released the girl, who instantly sank down upon the chair, half dead with excitement and emotion and half-faint from the violence of her exertions. She sat with panting breath and staring eyes while the cat and the mouse process was repeated. This time, however, the major played the minor part.

No, gentle reader, the intruder was not, as you have surmised, Mornington. Certainly it may not be doubted but that brave paladin would have enjoyed to the full such an opportunity, but he was at present incapable of shaking anything or anybody. The newcomer was a stranger to Susan. He was a captain in the major's regiment who had been on leave of absence in London and had at that moment come to report his return.

"What do you mean, sir," thundered the young officer, red with wrath and astonishment, "by attacking this poor lady?"

"Sir Francis!" cried the major, recovering his wits so soon as he recognized his assailant. "Captain Bloundell," he went on, "how dare you lay hands on your superior officer? Your sword, sir," he commanded. "You are under arrest."

"You dog!" cried Sir Francis Bloundell hotly, a young man of birth, breeding and station, who felt an open contempt for his gross and brutal superior, "if you ask for my sword I'll give it to you in your heart."

"I'll have you before a court for this!" fumed the major.

"No, you won't," returned Bloundell. "We're alone together, and it's my word against yours.

In that case, which of us, think you, will be believed, you low-bred hound?"

"You forget that we've a witness."

"And I would lie you into hell, if I could," said Susan quickly, burning with what she had been subjected to. Again it was most unladylike, but Sir Francis did not withhold a glance of admiration from her.

"What were you doing to this young lady?" he asked.

"None of your business!" returned the major, "and I will not be bullied by one of my subordinates. Corporal of the guard!" he shouted.

"Now, you repeat that cry or say one word to the corporal of the guard when he comes or move from this room without my permission," cried Bloundell furiously excited, "and I swear to God I'll kill you where you stand."

"He offered me the deadliest of insults, sir," said Susan at this juncture. "I am a prisoner, weak, alone, helpless."

"Not when I am by."

"May God bless you for that, sir," she said gratefully.

"I know who you are, madam," continued the officer more formally, "and I am here to protect you."

"And well have you done it, sir. You came

in the nick of time," answered the girl, wondering who had raised up this protector for her, yet accepting without hesitation his proffer of assistance. She knew a gentleman when she saw one and here was one of Mornington's breed.

"And I am fortunate to have arrived so opportunely," he said.

"We'll see what your protection avails," interrupted the major. "The woman is a prisoner. Even you will hardly dare to interfere between the king and his prisoners. She goes back to the stockade now, by Heaven, and I'll settle with you presently."

Bloundell laughed at him, an irritating laugh, something after the fashion of Mornington's. Susan wondered for a moment if all the gentlemen of England employed that very annoying manner toward people whom they regarded as inferiors.

"What, sir," asked Bloundell, "you would not send a sick woman out of the hospital before she's well?"

"I would rather go anywhere than be subjected to his insults," said Susan most emphatically.

"He will not trouble you further, madam, I assure you."

"I will send her wherever I please," said the

major, boiling with rage at this cool defiance of his authority, "to hell, if necessary, and you, too, damn you, for a meddling, interloping fool. I'll fix you."

"Now, that's one place," returned Bloundell gravely, "that from this very morning I've solemnly made up my mind never to frequent, because I would be certain to see you there and it's all I can do to stand you in this life."

The major gritted his teeth and clenched his hands. What he would have said or done is not known, for at that moment the door opened and in came the corporal of the guard.

"Corporal of the guard," roared the major.

"Have a care what you do," whispered Bloundell warningly.

"Take this ——" (he used a vile word out of the camps) pointing to Susan, "back to the stockade."

"Oh, no, corporal," said Sir Francis Bloundell, stepping quickly between the soldier and his prey. "Major Weggard is mistaken. You will say to the officer of the guard, with the commanding officer's compliments, that the prisoner is to be immediately paroled in custody of Lord Aldenford, in whose behalf I am acting."

"Wait!" cried the major, "by whose authority do you presume to interfere?"

The corporal stared open-mouthed from one to the other.

"By that which even you, for all your exalted rank and station," went on the other mockingly, "are bound to respect."

"Whose? Whose?" thundered the older officer.

"The King's," answered Bloundell. "Here."

He handed his superior a folded paper. Had Major Weggard consulted his inclination he would have torn it into bits and thrown it to the floor, but this was a course to which he did not dare resort. With shaking fingers he opened it slowly. A glance or two made him master of its contents. He controlled himself with great difficulty.

"You're right," he mumbled at last. "I was mistaken. Corporal, tell the officer of the guard to see that the discharge is made out and the prisoner is allowed to go away."

If looks could have killed, he had struck Susan dead, and Captain Bloundell, too, at his feet, that moment.

"Very good, sir," said the mystified corporal, saluting and withdrawing.

"Madam," said the captain, "you are free, or will be in a moment."

"Thank God and you, sir."

"Nay, madam, the credit is Lord Aldenford's!"

"I thank him too, though I know him not."

"You shall know him presently. Are you well enough to travel a short distance?"

"Well enough!" exclaimed Susan. "I could travel to the end of the world to get away from him."

"Our journey will scarce take us that far."

"Do I exchange one prison for another?"

"Nay, you go to Alden."

Alden! She remembered that was the home of Mornington. Had he effected her release?

"Is that where Robert Mornington lives?" she asked.

"Yes, madam."

"He is well?"

"Somewhat indisposed—but not seriously," went on the captain, as he saw the woman lay her hand on her heart and go pale. "I am his friend. He waits you, and—"

"Let us go now—this instant!" said the girl, rising and reaching out a trembling hand.

"Allow me," he said, motioning her to her seat again. "We have something to do before we leave. Now, sir," he turned to the major, "you applied to this lady a moment since a word which I would not repeat in her presence, in the presence of any gentlewoman, and you insulted her grossly before you did so. You will get down on your knees and beg her pardon."

"And if I refuse?"

"You won't refuse," said the captain calmly.

"You are my subordinate," began the major feebly, "and I can—"

"You can do nothing. When you cease to be a gentleman you become inferior to the meanest private in the ranks, and if I choose to declare this shameful story you would be driven out of the army to the tune of the Rogue's March."

The major opened his mouth to protest, but the patience of the captain was exhausted. He caught him by the shoulder and, before he realized what he was doing, forced him down on his knees upon the floor.

"Apologize! Damn you!" he said ferociously, his hand on the back of the other's neck, choking him until his eyes nearly started from his head.

"I'm sorry," faltered the major.

"That will do, please," said Susan, interposing, fearful lest Bloundell would kill the man where he knelt.

The captain shook him off, struck him heavily on the cheek which Susan had not smitten, and threw him to the floor.

"You insulted me, too, and that's for it. Now, if you want any satisfaction, although you have no claim to being a gentleman, I may perhaps be prevailed upon to give it to you. It would be a pleasure to kill you. I have a carriage at the door," he said, turning to Susan coolly, and wiping his hands together as if to eliminate the contamination of the major's touch. "Have you any belongings?"

"None but these I have on, and they are not mine," said the girl.

The captain looked at her a moment appraisingly.

"They're poor stuff for a gentlewoman," he said, "but we'll soon remedy that."

He took out a couple of guineas, threw them viciously at the major, who still sat on the floor.

"Pay whoever furnished this stuff out of that," he said grandly. "Now, madam."

He offered her his arm, and Susan, feeling very faint and ill, yet wondrously relieved and happy, took it and accompanied him to the door.

CHAPTER XXVII

DELAY

HAD the captain consulted his desires he would
certainly have endeavored to beguile the tedium
of what to him was a familiar journey by engag-
ing his young companion in conversation, but he
had been strictly charged to tell her as little of
the circumstances that had led to her release as
he could, and to avoid, so far as was possible,
dwelling upon Mornington, his condition or his
plans. It was certainly hard lines for him, he
thought, placed in juxtaposition to this extraor-
dinary and charmingly beautiful girl, to be de-
barred from the advantages of his opportunities. But Bloundell was that rare thing in life,
a loyal friend. Susan, as he would have phrased
it, was the property of another. "Hands off"
was his motto.

The young lady herself was naturally deeply
grateful to her vigorous and effective protector.
He had arrived most opportunely for her—such

matters being more easily arranged in novels than in life, by the way, although they do really happen with sufficient frequency in real life to justify the writer. She shuddered to think from what his advent had freed her, and there were no bounds to the thanksgivings on her lips and in her heart. But such is the singular selfishness of women in love—and the quality is perhaps more apparent in men in the same circumstances —that the remembrance of these services, great and vital though they were, was lost in the knowledge that Mornington was well; that he had thought of her; that she was going to him.

Indeed, when they entered the carriage, she had straightway questioned the captain upon these points, finding him strangely reticent and unwilling to discuss anything or to impart any information, save that she already enjoyed. He had told her that Alden was only a short distance from Weymouth; that an hour's drive would bring her to the Hall. She had only, therefore, to repress her soul's impatience until that journey had been made, and all she hoped would be made clear to her, yet to repress her soul's impatience was perhaps, under the circumstances, the hardest task that had been set to her since she had dragged Mornington through the surf on the day of the wreck.

They passed by the scene of that memorable adventure on the way to the Hall, and Susan surveyed the melancholy remains of the brave ship that had been her only home for so many years with a certain languid interest, languid because Susan could not really feel much interest in anything except Mornington at that moment. She wanted to see him so badly that her vision was indifferent to everything else, including Captain Bloundell, which somewhat piqued that enterprising and spirited young man. In her weak condition Susan had no room for a great variety of emotions. She could support but one subject of attention. Mornington had not come to her, but she was going to him. She would see him. That would suffice for the present. Only to look at him would satisfy her now, she thought.

Finally she leaned back in the comfortable carriage and closed her eyes to dream, but not to sleep, to shut out everything but the picture of him imprinted upon her heart. In this manner the two ill-assorted travelers reached the Hall. Susan saw before her a somewhat dilapidated Elizabethan castle of noble architecture. Some of it appeared habitable, but the major portion was in a state of extreme decay. A broad flight of steps rose from the drive, shaded by noble oaks, to the terrace upon which the mansion was

built, and from the terrace another flight of steps
led to the great entrance hall, in the door of
which stood a venerable and dignified figure in
modest, if somewhat worn, livery.

Sir Francis assisted Susan to descend from the
carriage, helped her carefully up the long flight
of steps, supported her gently across the terrace
and into the door of the hall.

"Good morning, Sir Francis," began the man
who stood in the doorway.

"Ah, Packingham," said Sir Francis cheerfully, "how is your master?"

"His lordship is doing very well, indeed, sir,
considering all things, and have you—?"

"Yes, this is the young lady.   Will he see her
now, think you?"

"Sir Francis," was the answer, "he has been
in a fever of impatience ever since we carried
him into the house."

"I beg your pardon," began Susan falteringly
—she had not the slightest interest in Lord Aldenford—"but I am so tired, and—"

"A thousand pardons," exclaimed Sir Francis
contritely, "I forgot how ill you had been.   A
chair, Packingham, and a glass of wine for the
lady."

All solicitude, the officer assisted Susan into
the great hall and sat her down before a fireplace

in which huge logs were burning cheerfully, while Packingham, the butler, ran for some light refreshment.

"Now, Sir Francis," said the servant, "we have been expecting you and his lordship wants to see the young lady as soon as is convenient to her, sir."

Susan had partaken of the glass of rare old port which the faithful servant handed to her, and she felt greatly refreshed by the generous wine.

"I beg your pardon, sir," she said to her escort, "but you told me that Lieutenant Mornington was here and I gathered that he was not well. Indeed, it must be so, else he would have taken your place."

"Mornington!" exclaimed the old servant, apparently greatly surprised at this simple statement.

"Is he not here?" asked Susan piteously, noting the old man's amazement.

"Yes, yes, certainly," said Captain Bloundell, shaking his head at the astonished butler, and if Susan had been observant she could have seen that the officer distinctly winked at the man. "Of course, you shall see him directly, but this place belongs to Lord Aldenford. You know he is the head of the house, and—"

"Is he related to Lieutenant Mornington?" asked the girl.

"Certainly, very nearly, and I think it would perhaps be just as well to see him first."

"But I want to see Robert—Mr. Mornington —right away. I can't wait. I—"

"My dear lady," insisted Bloundell gently, "this, I am afraid, is a case where you will have to heed the wishes of his lordship."

"You are keeping something from me," cried the girl. "Lieutenant Mornington is not here. He is ill—dead!"

"I give you my word," answered Sir Francis quickly, "that he is here, and while he is not particularly well, I am sure he soon will be. But now you must ask me no more questions. You shall see him some time to-day without fail. Indeed, I think I may say it is his wish that you should see Lord Aldenford first."

"Very well, then," said Susan, at once acquiescent. "I don't understand, but if he wishes it—"

"By Heavens!" thought Bloundell, "what a lucky dog Bob is, to be sure! The girl is absolutely willing to do anything for him, even on a mere intimation from me that he wants it. Well, he's a good fellow, but, hang him! I wish I'd seen her first. Some men do have all the luck.

I'm glad I slapped that beggar Weggard, though!"

Susan rose to her feet and signified her willingness for the audience with Lord Aldenford. She could not understand why Mornington had not come to her or allowed her to go to him, but if it were his wish, that was enough for her.

"I beg your pardon, my lady—ma'am, I mean," began Packingham, who was evidently chief factotum of the castle, "but Lord Aldenford had me lay out some clothes, dresses and furbelows which he had brought from London, thinking your wardrobe might have been lost in the ship, and—"

"I want nothing," said Susan impatiently, "but to get this interview over, so that I can see—"

"But, madam;" began Bloundell, "if Lord Aldenford wishes—"

"I care nothing whatever about his wishes."

"But if Mornington should express a desire?"

"That were different. But clothes would matter nothing to him. He has seen me in simpler guise than this, and, in short, if I am to see his lordship it must be this way or not at all."

For once the appeal to Mornington's influence apparently had failed.

"Oh, very well then," said Sir Francis, and

Packingham, to whom had been due the suggestion largely, made no further objection.

"Where is his lordship?"

"In the library, ma'am."

"Conduct me there at once, then," said the girl.

"Gad!" remarked Sir Francis to himself, "she's to the manor born all right, if she is an American. The way she ordered Packingham about reminds me of nothing so much as the captain of a ship."

"Sir," said Susan, turning to Bloundell, "shall I see you here when I return?"

"That you will," returned the young man heartily. "I am Lord Aldenford's best friend, and I told him I would see the thing through for his sake, but now that I have seen you, allow me to say, madam, that it needs no word from him. I should see it through for your own, and I am only sorry that I didn't have the first chance."

All of which was Greek to poor Susan.

"I am very grateful to you," she remarked, "and I shall hope to convey my thanks and gratitude to you in our better acquaintance, if indeed a prisoner is to have any rights that are to be respected."

She stretched out her hand to him, and Sir Francis bowed over it like the gallant gentleman that he was, and kissed it ere he relinquished it.

Susan felt no emotions of any sort at this pressure of the lips. Singular what a difference it makes whose lips are pressed upon the hand!

Her adieus being made, she stepped to the library door, beside which Packingham stood, drawn up in rigid and dignified immobility. As she approached he threw the door open grandly, and then first remembered that he knew not the lady's name.

"I beg your pardon, ma'am"—he barred the way when she would have entered—"but will you kindly give me your name?"

"Hubbell, Susan Hubbell," answered the girl.

Packingham looked aghast at the combination, but recovered himself in due time, and roared it through that great baronial hall, as if it had been one of the dukes or duchesses of the olden time.

"Miss Susan Hubbell," he cried in an astonishingly deep voice, "to see Lord Aldenford."

"Gad!" murmured Sir Francis, watching the scene back in the hall, "it's a good thing that she's got beauty to compensate for that Susan. However, half of the name will soon be changed, or I'm no judge. Lucky Bob!"

And so the door closes upon him and he exits from this truthful history as he steps out upon the walk to reflect upon his bad fortune in having met Susan too late!

CHAPTER XXVIII

CORONET AND COIN

THE room which Susan entered was a tall, vaulted apartment, lined with books and very imperfectly lighted by small old windows filled with leaded glass. A solitary individual, a man, was sitting in a great chair at the upper end near a desk. The man rose to his feet as Susan approached him.

"My lord," she began as she drew near. Half way down the room she stopped and threw out her arms with an exclamation.

"Mr. Mornington!" she cried, "Robert!"

It was indeed he. She saw now why he had not come to the stockade to help her in person, why he had not been at the door to greet her. His arm was in a sling; his head was bandaged; he was deathly pale, and he swayed with weakness where he stood, supporting himself by the side of the desk.

Her own weakness was forgotten at the moment. With a great rush of love and pity she ran toward him. She slipped her arm around his neck and with his remaining arm he pressed her to his breast. Again the little scene in the cabin was repeated. Their surroundings fled away from him and from her. With the meeting of their lips they stepped into Arcadia, hand in hand, arm in arm—the world forgetting, surely; and by the world forgot, as well.

Susan clung to him, sobbing, crying, laughing, kissing him again and again, and in spite of his bodily weakness he found strength somewhere to return every caress in full measure. There was a broad sofa before the fire. Had it been placed there for this purpose by the considerate Packingham, I wonder? These two poor children, at any rate, finally sat down upon it, side by side, hand in hand, and babbled those sweet nothings which have been the stock of lovers and the sport of story tellers—and story readers, too—since time and the world began.

Coherency, cogency, logical sequence, are not looked for at such moments. Although it cause the fair reader deep disappointment, the chronicler will not attempt to draw aside the veil and reveal all that happened then. It was not until some time later that he permits himself to take up the thread of his discourse.

"My heart broke," said the girl, "when you were stricken down on the deck in my arms. It broke again when I found they had taken you away from me, and it broke worse than all when they told me you had been at the hospital to see me and had gone."

"That little article you refer to must be pretty well in shivers by this time," commented Mornington with some resumption of his former air.

"It's well now," she said. "The first kiss that you gave me mended it all."

"It strikes me that that kiss I received rather than gave," laughed the happy lieutenant.

"I don't care. You can't mock me now, and perhaps I would rather give than receive."

"That's Scriptural, at any rate," returned her lover, "but you don't mean by that that you don't want my kisses?"

Her answer was an ample demonstration of the negative of that proposition. Does the gentle reader wonder that I refrain from entering further into the details of the scene? I should bring the blush of shame to his or her cheek, because under such circumstances people invariably act the same way. They are all foolish. Although there may be degrees of foolishness, there is none of low degree under such condition.

"Tell me," began Susan again—when it is safe

to take up the thread of this much punctuated discourse—"why you left me without a word?"

"I had business."

"What business? A woman's?"

"You have defined it."

Susan drew away.

"What woman?"

"One I used to think a great deal of, and—"

"What is her name? Do you care for her now? Was it to break it off with her in preparation for this? What did she say?"

"One question at a time," answered Mornington. "I loved her some time ago and it was in preparation for this that I went away."

"Couldn't you stay one hour till I awakened?" queried Susan jealously, drawing farther away from him.

"Not a moment."

"What did you say her name was? Is she very beautiful?"

"Certainly, she is very beautiful, and her name is—"

"What? What?"

"Susan."

"Susan!" cried the girl, "why, that's my name!"

"And you were the woman."

"You had business with me?"

"With His Majesty, the King, my darling. I had to get you out of that prison, and there was no way of accomplishing it save by securing a personal order from the King himself. I galloped up to London, presented myself to him in all my romantic disarray—"

"You poor boy! How brave of you!" she interrupted, rewarding him sweetly as woman can.

"Thank you," he went on. "I told him about the loss of the ship, your heroic rescue of me, which I learned from the sergeant, your detention in prison and of your illness. And I begged His Majesty to pardon you the crime of rebellion and permit me to take you away on my promise of being responsible for your behavior. Incidentally, I assured His Majesty that I intended to marry you at the earliest possible moment."

"And do you think that would insure my good behavior, sir?" cried Susan, happy over that last announcement.

"I am certain of it," he answered confidently.

"And you went up to London before you were able to travel, for me?"

"I wanted to go the moment I regained consciousness, but they absolutely held me in the bed."

"And why didn't you come yourself to the prison this morning?"

"After I had got what I went for," said Mornington, "I utterly collapsed. They brought me back in a traveling carriage. Fortunately I met Frank Bloundell and he would not hear of my undertaking the release, he promised to do it himself, so they brought me here. They say I should be in bed now, but I give you my word, Miss Susan Hubbell, I never felt better in my life."

"You look it," said the girl, smiling tenderly upon him. "Now I shall nurse you back to health."

"And who, pray, will nurse my poor, wasted, worn, tired darling?"

"We'll nurse each other," she said, laughing in pure joy. "Indeed, indeed, Robert, it only wanted this to make me well."

She lifted his hand and pressed it against her faithful, devoted heart as she spoke.

"How did Bloundell acquit himself of his errand?" he asked presently.

"Like a hero, like a gentleman."

"You must not think too much of him. I shall be jealous. He is a very fascinating fellow."

"I don't. He is nothing compared to you, but he did as well as he could."

And then she told him quickly all that had happened.

"I wish that I had been there!" he said, "but Frank certainly made good use of his opportunities. I am eternally grateful to him."

"And I, too."

"As for Major Weggard, he shall be dismissed from the army at once. Now, there is one thing more, one other business that I had in London."

"And what was that?"

"It's this," he answered, drawing from the pocket of his coat a paper which he handed to her. She opened it and looked at it.

"Why!" she said, as her mind puzzled itself over the unfamiliar phraseology, "it seems to be a marriage license made out for Susan Hubbell and Robert Cecil Mornington, Earl of Aldenford." She dropped the paper. "You!" she exclaimed, "a lord!"

"I am indeed one of those unfortunate beings," returned his lordship equably.

"Why didn't you tell me so on the ship?"

"I had an idea that you people in America had conceived a prejudice against lords, and I thought it just as well to sink the title in my family name. Does it make any difference?" he questioned anxiously before her startled gaze.

"None," said the girl frankly, "nothing could make any difference to me now that I love you."

"And you will marry me?"

"Immediately. Whenever you like."

"It shall be to-day then," he answered joyfully. "But before you become My Lady I must tell you something about myself."

"There is nothing you could tell me," she interrupted, "that would make the slightest difference. I know you better than you know yourself, indeed, and you are wasting words that you might use"—she bent toward him—"in making love to me."

"Susan," he said severely, "this is no time to trifle. I have sad news to communicate."

"What is that?"

"I am a poor man."

"You own this castle?"

"It is mortgaged to its full value. I don't suppose there is a peer of England that has less money, and when I look at you I add more luck, than I have. But I am absolutely dependent, or almost so, upon my profession. I am offering you an ancient name and a high title, but a lean purse. Does that make any difference?"

"Of course not," said Susan, greatly relieved at his disclosure. "I should marry you if you had nothing, not even a name."

Mornington thanked her in the most approved method.

"'Now," she said, "I, too, have a confession to make."

"Look here, Susan," he began anxiously, "if it's to tell me that you have ever had any love affair with any other man, will you please seek some other time to disclose the painful fact?"

"Your only rival in my affections," began the girl, "was my good, kind, noble father. No, my confession is of another kind. I come before you apparently as penniless as even you profess yourself to be, but I must admit that I really have some money laid by."

"I thought that you lost everything in the *Hiram and Susan*—the sweetest ship and the luckiest for me that ever sailed the seas."

"I didn't though," said the girl. "My grandfather was one of the richest merchants of Boston. He left it all to my father and now it has come to me. I shall not come to you a penniless bride. I suppose that perhaps I am worth in money, in land, in ships, nearly a hundred thousand pounds."

"You are simply priceless," exclaimed Mornington, taking her again to his heart; "you could not estimate your worth in any precious commodity known to earth or heaven!"

*   *   *   *   *   *

There was a quiet wedding at the Hall that

day. Bloundell was the best man at the ceremony. His sister, summoned from the adjoining country place, obligingly stood up with Susan, and Mr. Bob Young, boatswain, formerly in the United States service, brought from the stockade by the influence of My Lord Aldenford, gave away the blushing bride.

And there stands "The Blue Ocean's Daughter," transplanted to Merry England and become the Countess of Aldenford, clinging to her husband's arm, looking out upon a new and strange life with a serene and happy confidence begot of the tried quality of her husband's affection and the abounding depth of her own feeling. And there we say "Good-bye" to them.

THE END